"You are not doing this to be kind?"

Maria asked.

Mitch shook his head, his voice gruff when he answered, "No."

She met his gaze, a look of unspeakable awe in her face. "I will take very good care, Mitchell, I promise," she said in a hushed tone.

To be so awed by the little apartment he'd agreed to let her live in—what kind of life had she had?

"Here, check this out. See what you think of the view."

She came over to stand beside him, and he suddenly wished she didn't smell like gardenias. He had to close his eyes and fight the air as his heartbeat faltered.

Getting a grip, he moved away, the scent of gardenias following him.

Too close. He had let her get too close. But a little voice in his head disputed that. No, it said, not nearly close enough.

Dear Reader,

Once again, Silhouette Intimate Moments brings you an irresistible lineup of books, perfect for curling up with on a winter's day. Start with Sharon Sala's *A Place To Call Home,* featuring a tough city cop who gets away to the Wyoming high country looking for some peace and quiet. Instead he finds a woman in mortal danger and realizes he has to help her—because, without her, his heart will never be whole.

For all you TALL, DARK AND DANGEROUS fans, Suzanne Brockmann is back with *Identity: Unknown.* Navy SEAL Mitchell Shaw has no memory of who—or what—he is when he shows up at the Lazy 8 Ranch. And ranch manager Becca Keyes can't help him answer those questions, though she certainly raises another: How can he have a future without her in it? Judith Duncan is back with *Marriage of Agreement,* a green-card marriage story filled with wonderful characters and all the genuine emotion any romance reader could want. In *His Last Best Hope,* veteran author Susan Sizemore tells a suspenseful tale in which nothing is quite what it seems but everything turns out just the way you want. With her very first book, New Zealander Fiona Brand caught readers' attention. *Heart of Midnight* brings back Gray Lombard and reunites him with the only woman strong enough to be his partner for life. Finally, welcome Yours Truly author Karen Templeton to the line. *Anything for His Children* is an opposites-attract story featuring three irresistible kids who manage to teach both the hero and the heroine something about the nature of love.

Enjoy every one of these terrific novels, and then come back next month for six more of the best and most exciting romances around.

Yours,

Leslie J. Wainger
Executive Senior Editor

Please address questions and book requests to:
Silhouette Reader Service
U.S.: 3010 Walden Ave., P.O. Box 1325, Buffalo, NY 14269
Canadian: P.O. Box 609, Fort Erie, Ont. L2A 5X3

MARRIAGE OF AGREEMENT

JUDITH DUNCAN

Published by Silhouette Books

America's Publisher of Contemporary Romance

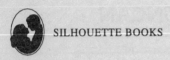 SILHOUETTE BOOKS

ISBN 0-373-07975-3

MARRIAGE OF AGREEMENT

Copyright © 1999 by Judith Mulholland

Visit us at www.romance.net

Printed in U.S.A.

Books by Judith Duncan

Silhouette Intimate Moments

A Risk Worth Taking #400
Better Than Before #421
*Beyond All Reason #536
*That Same Old Feeling #577
*The Return of Eden McCall #651
Driven to Distraction #704
Murphy's Child #946
Marriage of Agreement #975

Silhouette Books

To Mother with Love 1993
"A Special Request"

*Wide Open Spaces

JUDITH DUNCAN

is married and lives, along with two of her five children and her husband, in Calgary, Alberta, Canada. A staunch supporter of anyone wishing to become a published writer, she has lectured at several workshops for Alberta's Department of Culture and participated in conventions in both British Columbia and Oregon. After having served a term as 2nd Vice President for the Canadian Authors' Association, she is currently working with the Alberta Romance Writers' Association, which she helped to found.

To Donna Levia
Thanks for the solution.

Chapter 1

February 20

The brightly lit departure-level concourse of Calgary International Airport echoed with the clatter of luggage carts and the clamor of voices, the steady din abruptly overridden by a flight departure announcement over the PA system.

A lineup of vacant-faced passengers snaked through a cordoned pathway, their movements made sluggish and cumbersome by heavy winter clothes. It was as if they, too, were oppressed by the noise. The vast space was a gigantic conduit for the steady racket, moving it like a living thing from one end of the concourse to the other.

Behind the barrier created by kiosks and small shops, the cavernous passenger lounge was oddly quiet, as if muffled by the faded, eerie light seeping in from outside. It was as if the dull, gloomy day had oppressed the waiting room area, the heaviness of the weather creating a false silence. The February grayness seemed to suck out all the color, leaving everything and everybody in a dreary monochrome.

Falling snow swirled against the floor-to-ceiling windows, the fat, wet flakes sticking to the glass, then sliding down in trails of moisture. And the only colors in the gray-and-white landscape outside were the pink puddles of deicing fluid and the dark blue coveralls of the ground crews.

Mitchell Munroe undid the snaps of his fleece-lined denim jacket, then settled in the last seat in the row of bolted-down chairs closest to the windows, his damp jeans adding to his irritation. He'd had to go out and plug the meter again, and one hotdogging van had managed to catch him as it plowed through a puddle of water, soaking him from the hip down. One more last straw to add to the growing pile.

His aggravation level was mostly about his own foul-up. His mother had left a message on his voice mail the night before, asking to be picked up with a van, rather than a car. Since he owned the only cargo van in the entire family, and since he'd been the one to send them on a winter's vacation to Mexico in the first place, he was logically the one tagged for the job.

Which was okay by him. He didn't mind picking them up; he'd more or less planned on doing it anyway. What ticked him off was the lateness of their flight. He could think of fifteen things he'd rather be doing than wasting time here at the airport. But it was his own damned fault; he should have checked the airport channel on TV before he left work. But oh, no, not him. He'd been running late as it was, and he'd had to reinstall the back seat in the van, and he hadn't wanted to waste any more time. And now he was paying for it. The plane was late.

Trying to clamp down on another flare of irritation, he stretched his long legs out in front of him, then took a sip from the steaming foam cup he'd picked up from the doughnut shop, savoring the dark, rich flavor. At least the coffee was decent, and Lord knew he needed a caffeine refueling. He'd been going dead out since five that morning, when the greenhouse warning alarm had gone off.

Owning a successful tree farm, plant nursery and garden center was not without plenty of headaches. The heating system in one of the greenhouses had gone haywire, and the temperature had dropped, setting off the alarm. Of course, the problem had to be in one of the greenhouses in use—the one that held all the tropical and flowering plants.

It was a good thing Mitch lived in an apartment on the second floor of the huge barn-shaped garden center, and had been there to pick up the alarm. It would have really burned his butt if he'd lost several truckloads of fragile merchandise. But one good thing—at least it hadn't been minus thirty-eight degrees outside with a blizzard blowing, or he could have lost the whole shebang. In those kinds of bitter conditions, the temperature in a greenhouse could plunge to below zero in minutes. Yep, it could have been worse. A whole lot worse.

Mitch took another sip of coffee, then slouched down in his seat and hooked his ankle across his knee.

Actually, he shouldn't be whining about anything. He'd been damned lucky all around. Great summer and spring businesswise, with a reasonably mild winter so far. And on top of all that, his garden center and greenhouses had had an excellent Christmas season— the best ever. And Valentine's Day had been an absolute blowout. In fact, he'd had a terrific year.

At this very moment, his accountant, who also happened to be his sister-in-law, was back in his offices doing his books. And from the figures she'd been churning out when he left, it looked even better than he'd expected. Which meant he could afford to keep all his staff on payroll until spring, when it got busy again. And he was damned grateful for that. If there was one thing he hated above all else, it was having to lay off employees. He hadn't had to do it for a lot of years, and he hoped he never would. He had six people on permanent staff—a hard-working, dependable bunch—and he would never have seen the ongoing profits he had if it hadn't been for them. Yeah, they appreciated their Christmas bonuses, but with families to raise and mortgages to pay, they appreciated that regular paycheck even more, he knew.

Shifting to ease the discomfort of wet jeans, Mitch grasped his cup of coffee, then pulled the cuff of his jacket back with his middle finger to check his watch. Barring total whiteout conditions or a spontaneous blizzard, the plane should be touching down in fifteen minutes. Another twenty for his parents to clear Canadian customs…with any luck, he should be out of there in half an hour.

Resigning himself to another thirty minutes at least, he let his gaze sweep across the kiosks that bordered the waiting area, his attention snagging on the big blond dude standing beside a display rack, flipping through one of the magazines.

The guy was wearing a long, dark oilskin slicker and flat-crowned black cowboy hat, his too-long hair shaggy around the ears. In that getup, with his stand-out-in-a-crowd height and wide shoulders, he looked like some sort of outlaw. He had classic Nordic features, giving him the profile of a Viking warlord, as well as the jawline of an Irish pugilist and the stance of a gunslinger. And he had cocky written all over him.

As Mitch watched, two women pulling suitcases and wearing flight attendant uniforms passed by, one of them swiveling right around to get a good long look at the big blonde.

A flicker of amusement lifted one corner of Mitch's mouth. Some things never changed. It was a wonder she hadn't dislocated her neck.

Mr. Macho turned and stuffed the magazine back in the rack; then he, too, checked his watch. Looking as antsy as Mitch felt, he crossed the concourse and entered the waiting area. He brushed past Mitch, snapping his fingers, then stopped in front of the row of windows. Pushing back his slicker, he jammed his hands in the back pockets of his blue jeans and stood staring out, his gaze fixed on the falling snow.

Mitch drank the last of his coffee and tossed the empty cup in a garbage receptacle. Then, resting his elbows on the chrome arms, he laced his hands across his chest and looked up. "Can't you at least afford a haircut?"

The blonde grinned and rocked back on his heels. "Feeling a little snarly, or are you always this rude?"

The corner of Mitch's mouth lifted just a little. "You look like an outlaw."

Murphy Munroe turned, the laugh lines around his eyes creasing. "You just can't stand it, can you—that I'm so much better looking than you?"

Mitch shook his head, restraining a smile. There might be fifteen months difference in their ages, but even he was aware—and he was hardly ever aware of any of those kinds of subtleties—that he and his brother could pass for twins. And in their younger, wilder years, had. In fact, if the light was bad, their grandmother still got them mixed up—and Baba wasn't one to mix anything up.

Mitch's tone was dry when he responded. "Don't you ever get tired of packing that great big ego around?"

Murphy chuckled and turned slightly, resting his shoulder against the window. "I gotta do something to pass the time." A restlessness radiated from him as he abruptly straightened and glanced at his watch again. "Do you suppose the plane is finally on the ground?"

Mitch snorted. "What are you complaining about? You've only been here ten minutes."

Murphy cast his brother a half testy, half amused look. "Hey. Don't climb my frame because you didn't have the brains to check arrivals before you drove all the way out here. That was not very swift, bro." He started snapping his fingers again. "I've had enough of standing here watching it snow. I'm going to head downstairs."

More than ready for a change of scene himself, Mitch stood up, rotating his torso to work the kinks out of his spine. He picked up some change that had fallen out of his pocket, then straightened. "Yeah. We may as well go check it out. With them flying first class, maybe we'll get lucky, and they'll be the first ones off."

"Yeah, right," Murphy responded, his tone thick with skepticism. "You know Ma. She'll have to make sure every little old lady, orphan of the storm and stray dog are taken care of before she'll check through. Traveling with her is like traveling with a damned welfare agency."

Mitchell gave a reluctant grin. His brother had that dead-on. Ellen Munroe figured it was her duty to mother the entire world.

They took the escalator to the arrival area on the lower concourse, and from that elevated vantage point, Mitch got a clear view of the Canada Customs check-through area. It was jammed with people, all waiting for incoming flights. He let go a weary sigh of resignation. Well, hell. That shot his early optimism to smithereens. That jam was a good indicator there was either an international jumbo jet due in, or more than one flight coming through customs at once. Which meant it was probably going to take a whole lot longer than half an hour.

He followed Murphy off the escalator, letting him break trail as they headed toward the stainless steel barriers surrounding a large open area in front of the frosted sliding doors. As Mitch followed his brother through the press of people, he tried to shrink into himself. God, but he hated crowds. With all the milling bodies and the babble from hundreds of voices, he felt as if he were surrounded by swarms of bees.

They finally found a clear space along the far wall, under the bright murals promoting the national parks located in Alberta. Hooking his thumbs in the front pockets of his jeans, Mitch leaned back against the wall, his gaze snagging on two women, wearing traditional white Stetsons, white shirts and red vests, who were circulating through the crowd. Calgary hospitality on the move. He'd heard once that the official greeters were all volunteers. A perfect job for his mother.

"There is not one damned thing funny about this," Murphy stated, his tone bordering on cranky. "So what are you smiling about?"

Mitch lifted his chin toward one of the hostesses. "I was just thinking. We should buy Ma a white hat and red vest and turn her loose out here. She'd be in seventh heaven."

Murphy's eyes lightened and a bad-boy grin appeared. "Don't you be mocking our mother, Mitchell Andrew," he said, perfectly mimicking their dead grandfather's Irish brogue. "She'll be nailing your wee shoes to the floor if you do."

Mitch cast his brother a cryptic look, then shifted his gaze back to the crowd. His height gave him a pronounced advantage, and he watched the milling people, the vivid-colored hats and scarves shifting like bright blossoms, the brightly hued ski jackets and dark-toned coats creating a sea of moving color. The scene reminded him of an impressionist painting.

A small giggling child with shiny black hair and black eyes dodged through the cluster of people standing directly in front of Mitchell. The child was being pursued by an older girl who was scolding the boy in Spanish. His expression sobering, Mitch watched them, wondering how his parents' trip had gone.

His mother had given him no indication in the message left on his voice mail, and he had made a point not to grill any of his siblings who had actually talked to their parents during their month-long holiday. He truly hoped this holiday hadn't been one big mistake.

The first-class airline tickets to Mexico had been a Christmas gift, given under the guise of a winter vacation. But that wasn't the real reason Mitch had sent his folks south.

For years and years his parents had sponsored foster kids in Latin America through a church-based organization. He had no idea how many, but there had been one who'd stood out among the crowd, one who had been different from the rest, one who had been special.

He'd been about fifteen—hell, which made it twenty-five years ago—when Maria had come into their care. His parents had heard about her from a Child Care Mission worker who had returned to Calgary, and her story had broken his mother's heart and fortified his father's. She'd been orphaned when she was two years old, left with her blind, crippled grandmother.

Owning nothing, the two of them had somehow survived the slums of the largest city in the world. She was nearly five years old when the Munroes first heard her story, and by then, the situation had deteriorated to the point where the child was practically the sole provider for her very frail grandmother. So his parents had made arrangements through the foster organization to provide private financial help for both of them, making sure that Maria and her grandmother got not only proper food and clothing and decent housing, but that the child got the best education available.

And that was how it had all started. But unlike other foster situations, perhaps because it had been arranged privately, this association never ended. And although Maria had never been physically part of the Munroe family, she had always been a presence.

Well aware that being able to speak English was going to give the girl opportunities she would never have otherwise, they made arrangements for her to take language instruction from the priest at the Catholic mission school. She'd been a beautiful, somber-eyed child, and in every one of the pictures that had been sent to the Munroes, she always looked so much older than her years. Reports from the school and the priest had always stated what a good student she was and how eager to learn. How she excelled in her English lessons. And without fail, she faithfully wrote.

Even after she started working for wealthy Americans vacationing in the area, and even after she was married at the age of seventeen, she continued to write long detailed letters to the Munroes. Such a connection had been established that one of Mitchell's three sisters even learned Spanish.

And when Maria married Pedro Rodriguez thirteen years ago, his parents had flown down for the ceremony. At the time, they'd worried about the union. Pedro had been over twenty years older than Maria, with two very small boys, and the Munroes had concerns about that. They had hoped for more for her. But Pedro passed inspection and was, in fact, awarded an

A rating from Patrick Munroe. And the connection continued.

When Maria's grandmother died a year later, the senior Munroes had gone down for the funeral, as well. In some strange, long-distance way, Maria had been assimilated into the family—another daughter, another distant sister. Just like the rest of the Munroe kids, there had been a progression of pictures of her displayed on the family piano. And the exotic-looking child eventually turned into an exotic-looking young woman.

Only somewhere along the way, the lines of communication started breaking down.

Maria's husband had died two years before, after a long bout with cancer, and from the time he'd taken ill, things had started to change. They'd heard from Maria less and less frequently, but the Munroes had assumed it was because of the terrible strain she was under.

When Ellen and Patrick Munroe got word from the mission priest that Pedro Rodriguez had died, they'd planned on flying down immediately. But Maria had been adamant. Through the priest, she'd asked them to please not come, and they had abided by her wishes. But Mitch had wondered at the time why she hadn't wanted them there. After Pedro's death, Maria's letters had become even more infrequent and noticeably less chatty, until they stopped coming altogether. Ellen Munroe worried constantly about her. She didn't want to intrude if Maria didn't want her there, but she had continued to worry nevertheless. It had been damned hard on his mother.

Mitch had been to Mexico on business a few times

himself, and he'd toyed with the idea of making a side trip to check things out. But Maria didn't know him from Adam's off ox, and besides, he really didn't want to get involved. He'd made a career out of not getting involved.

Mitch expelled a long breath and straightened, sticking his hands in the front pockets of his jeans. But he wasn't so removed that he didn't occasionally wonder about the situation. He was aware that he was sometimes as thick as a plank about picking up vibes, but this time he had definitely picked up on his mother's. Clear as a bell. In fact, he had a feeling he was the only one who had clued in to his mother's worry.

So without saying anything to anybody, he had made the decision to do something about it. And he'd taken matters into his own hands, getting his parents airline tickets as a Christmas present. A winter holiday in Mexico. Even Maria couldn't argue with that. And since they were already there, why not a side trip to visit their foster daughter? How could Maria object? At least, that had been his rationale. But he had to admit his rationale sometimes got him the same results as spitting into the wind.

Suddenly realizing that he and Murphy were standing in the exact same pose—shoulder to shoulder, feet spread, arms folded across their chests as they stared straight ahead, just like a pair of beer hall bouncers— Mitch moved. He grinned to himself. Man, sometimes their physical sameness even buzzed *him* out.

Almost as if sensing the imminent appearance of passengers from the Customs area, the crowd began clustering around the barricades, and Mitch shifted position again. If somebody didn't walk through that damned door pretty soon, he was going to start bouncing something, all right, preferably some Customs official's head.

As if electronically plugged into his thought processes, the frosted doors slid open, disgorging one lone male passenger pushing a loaded luggage cart, a long thin duffel holding skis atop his baggage. Taking advantage of the audience pressed around the barriers, the kid grinned and swept off his vivid purple-and-yellow jester-style ski cap, then gave the crowd an exaggerated bow. There was a buzz of laughter, and some of the crowd clapped. Folding his arms, Mitch studied the kid. He wasn't sure he could remember ever being that young.

The door slid open again, releasing another group of people from the bowels of Canada Customs, and Mitch stuck his hands back in his pockets, fighting the need to pace. At this speed, they would still be here at midnight.

It wasn't midnight. But it was pitch-black outside—at 20:47, to be exact—his parents, suntanned and loaded down with twice as much baggage as they'd left with, finally appeared through the doors, sandwiched in the middle of a group of people.

As if joined at the hip, Mitch and Murphy both straightened, then started toward the opening in the barricade. Their mother spotted them, her face breaking into a huge smile. She left their father to struggle with both luggage carts, coming toward her sons with open arms.

She was something else, their mother. Mitch might be forty, but right then, he felt as if he were about nine years old. She hugged him hard, like she always did.

He hugged her back, his voice unexpectedly gruff when he spoke. "Welcome home, Ma."

She patted his cheek and turned to hug his brother. Looking very pleased with herself, she gave them another happy smile. "I am so glad you're both here. I can't tell you how good it is to be back home."

Murphy chuckled, relieving her of her shoulder bag. "You might change your tune when you see what's going on outside, Ma. It ain't exactly the tropics."

She shook off his disclaimer. "I don't care. It's still good to be home."

Mitch stepped around her to help his father with one of the luggage carts. Patrick Munroe gave one son a bear hug, then the other. Stepping back, he shoved the cart back and forth. "Why is it," he said, half perplexed, half annoyed, and clearly wanting to swear but restraining himself, "that I always get a cart with one square wheel?"

Murphy grinned. "Because, Dad."

Taking the other cart, Mitch started toward the exit. "Come on. Let's get out of here. The van's this way."

His mother spoke, an odd tone in her voice. "Mitchell."

Mitch turned and saw a group of four people—all obviously Latino—herded together, standing like a group of wary hostages beside his father. As if drawn by a magnet, his gaze locked on a solemn-faced young woman with large dark eyes and a perfect oval face, her black hair pulled back in a thick braid. She was taller than most Latino women; the top of her head would probably clear his shoulder. And he found it disturbing, the way she held his gaze. There was something in her face, in the dark bottomless depths of her grave, unwavering eyes, that set off so many warning bells that danger signs started popping up in his head. His stomach shrank into a hard little ball, and for some inexplicable reason, he had the urge to back away.

His heart feeling suddenly too big for his chest, he forced himself to disconnect from that steady stare, and he shifted his gaze. Feeling as if he were standing in a long, narrow tunnel, he made a conscious effort to catalog the rest of the group—a bent old man with snow-white hair and gnarled hands, and two dark, handsome adolescent boys. Functioning in a kind of what's-going-on daze, Mitch gave his mother a blank look. There was a sparkle of expectation in her eyes, as if he was supposed to figure it all out on his own, as if she could barely contain her excitement. Wondering what in hell she was up to this time, he gave the group of four another quick perusal. Then all of a sudden the pieces slammed into place. He stared at the woman, a roller-coaster sensation sliding through his gut.

If he'd thought a trip to Mexico would satisfy his mother's high-revving maternal instinct, boy, had he been wrong.

Feeling as if he'd just stuck his finger in a live socket, he shot a stunned glance at his brother, who had the same poleaxed look as Mitch had. Suffering from a tingling sensation, Mitch somehow managed to force what he hoped was a reasonable facsimile of a composed expression onto his face. Well, he sure in hell didn't have to wonder what had happened in Mexico. Because the problem in Mexico was now here.

Those sensational, serious dark eyes staring back at him belonged to one Maria Rodriguez. And one other thing for sure, this wasn't just another photograph. This was the real live thing. Very real. And very live. He could smell the warmth of her skin from ten feet away.

It was a punch in the gut, but nevertheless a somewhat enlightening experience. For one thing, up until that moment, Mitch had had no idea he could actually function in a daze. But he could—and did. He figured his total mental lapse was because of the unexpected bomb his mother and father had dropped on them. Who brought an entire family home with them from a foreign country without saying one word to anyone? His parents, obviously.

Smiling that maternal smile of hers, his mother took Maria's hand and pulled her closer. "Of course you know Maria."

Which, Mitch mentally corrected, was not entirely true. All he knew of Maria was her smiling face from the top of his parents' piano. That hardly equated with the solemn, clearly nervous live person standing before him. Murphy spoke to her and shook her hand, but Mitch deliberately kept his own hands anchored in his pockets. He wasn't going there. Not in this lifetime.

Mitch wasn't sure how he managed to get through the introductions without doing anything stupid. But he did. Besides the very solemn, nervous Maria, there were her two teenage stepsons, Roberto and Enrico, sixteen and fourteen respectively. The boys also caught him off guard. He'd never expected their English to be just as fluent as their mother's. Hell, what was he thinking? He hadn't expected them at all.

The old man with the white hair and sharp, bright

eyes turned out to be Maria's seventy-eight-year-old father-in-law, also called Pedro. Pedro practically creaked with arthritis, spoke not-so-perfect English and had a surprising strength in his crippled handshake.

The unexpectedness of the situation left Mitch feeling as if he'd been caught in some kind of mental backwash, left stumbling around in a fog. Everything seemed totally out of focus. The babble of the crowd. The jumble of colors. The movement of his mother's mouth as she talked. Hell, the entire situation.

But in spite of that odd, disembodied sensation, he somehow managed to pull it together and act normal. It took some doing, but he and his brother eventually managed to get them all herded out to the van, where he and Murphy stowed all the luggage.

During the whole loading process, both his father and mother continued to act as if turning up with four Mexican citizens was the most normal thing in the world, and neither of them offered so much as a whisper of explanation. Mitch wasn't sure he even wanted one. Usually, at least with his family, it was much safer not knowing. Besides, it was none of his business. If his parents wanted to bring an entire Mexican village home to stay with them, that was their business. They were grown-ups. And they certainly didn't need permission from him. It was a hell of a lot safer simply not knowing.

And he got to keep his nose out sooner than expected. There was the matter of all those people and only one van. It only made sense that the two brothers would travel back together, leaving Patrick Munroe to drive the van. That suited Mitch just fine. In fact, he had suggested it. If he had a choice, he'd prefer to stay in the dark as long as possible.

Once in Murphy's truck, both brothers sat staring out the windshield, as if they'd been shot. Finally Murphy spoke. "Just what in hell was that all about?"

Suddenly too warm, Mitch roughly unsnapped his jacket. "Haven't a clue."

Shaking his head, Murphy reached down and turned on the ignition and headlights, then put the truck in reverse. "Well, whatever it is, it's sure one bloody big secret." Resting his arm across the back of the seat, he twisted around to look through the rear window as he backed the truck out. "You think they could have told us what they were up to, instead of just dumping it on us." Clear of the parking space, he changed gears and surged ahead. "All I can say is that thank God Jordan is meeting us at the house. I don't know about you, but I'm personally feeling like a damned duck, and someone just drained the pond."

Mitch knew exactly how his brother felt. He didn't like surprises. Never had. Never would. But knowing that Jordan was going to be at the house when they got there left him breathing just a little easier.

Jordan was Murphy's wife, and Mitch's accountant, and she had the rare talent of being able to read a situation and splice together loose ends so smoothly, it was as if there were no loose ends at all. He would be quite happy to dump the entire mess in Jordan's lap; he certainly had no intentions of touching it with a ten-foot pole. Jordan was all right. In fact, Mitch was far more comfortable with her than he was with any of his three sisters. His sister-in-law knew when not to push, and she also knew when to mind her own business. Yep, he'd stand back and let Jordan deal with it. He was simply going to reclaim his van and go home.

Like a kid with a bad report card in his pocket, Murphy didn't exactly break any records getting home. He abided by the speed limit to the letter. Actually, his brother drove like an aged old man. In spite of the queasy feeling in his gut, Mitch was amused. There was more than one way to stay out of the line of fire.

By the time they reached their parents' house, and their old home, there wasn't a soul in sight. Jordan Munroe's sports utility vehicle was parked on the street, and Mitch and Murphy exchanged a look of guilty relief.

She met them at the door, the light from inside framing her in the doorway. Even in faded sweats and her blond hair slipping from a discreet French fold— with a kid on one hip and one hanging off the other leg and her third pregnancy just beginning to show— she had this aura of elegance about her that never faltered. Murphy's wife was one classy lady.

She grinned as they came up the step. "My, my. Don't you two look as if you've just been launched out of a cannon." She straightened two-year old J.J.'s hair as his father bent to pick him up, then shifted year-old Eric higher on her hip. A knowing sparkle in her eyes, she gave Murphy a kiss. "And it took you long enough to get here. What did you do, come home through Cochrane?"

In spite of himself, Mitch grinned. "Not quite. But for the first time in his life, lover boy drove like a sane human being. Even stopped for orange lights."

She chuckled and patted her husband's cheek. "How cowardly of you, dear heart." Stepping back so they could enter, she motioned to the stack of luggage piled in the front hallway. "Okay. For starters. That pile is all the Rodriguezes' stuff, and everything goes downstairs. Your mother has decided they would all be more comfortable there, especially with the extra bedrooms and baths." She indicated a pile of boxes. "Those boxes go in Jessica's old room. And this," she said, indicating the pile off to one side, "is Mom's and Dad's, and it needs to go in their bedroom."

Mitch wasn't going anywhere near the Rodriguezes' stuff, and he sure as hell wasn't going downstairs. Toeing off his wet boots, he shut the door behind them, stepped over a cardboard box and hooked the strap of a carry-on over his shoulder, then picked up one large suitcase and a matching garment bag. The weight of the suitcase nearly pulled his arm right out of its socket. He started to swear, then remembered the presence of his small nephews. "Shi—oot, what have they got packed in these? Bricks?"

Murphy grinned and waggled his eyebrows at Mitch's recovery. Setting down his son, he reached for one of the boxes. "Serves you right for being such a chicken liver." He glanced at J.J. "Come on, little stuff. You can help Daddy."

Mitch made two trips to his parents' bedroom, and after returning from depositing the second load, he entered the kitchen. He found his mother there, making a pot of coffee. The Munroe kitchen, large and spacious, had always been the central point of the house. It was as if everything else revolved around that one, single room.

There was a large round table, which when fully extended could seat sixteen people, in the eating area in front of the patio doors. Beyond that, a huge work island featured a double sink at one end. And beyond that was the U-shaped work area, surrounded by cupboards. There were two built-in ovens, a double-wide fridge, along with a built-in microwave, another double sink, and a range top that had six burners rather than the usual four. A fireplace took up the end wall, with bookshelves on either side jammed with cookbooks. Healthy, lush plants were everywhere, including a bunch of tall tropical plants sitting in the corner on the terra cotta floor.

It was a kitchen designed for traffic, for convenience, and definitely to accommodate a big family. The rest of the house might change and serve other purposes, but Mitch always felt most at home in this room. It was the heart of the house—maybe even the heart of the whole family.

Only the recessed lighting under the cupboards was on, and the kitchen was cast in half-light, with shadows piling up against the vaulted ceiling. His mother looked tired, and there were new worry lines around her mouth. She glanced at her eldest son and stared at him an instant, then glanced back down at what she was doing. "Am I picking up on some disapproval, Mitchell?" she asked, her tone quiet.

Resting his hands on his hips, he looked squarely at her. "Ma, you aren't picking up on anything. It's none of my business."

She put the lid on the coffee canister, then set it back on the cupboard. "Perhaps. But something's got you by the shorts. I know that look."

He wasn't about to explain to anyone, especially his mother, what "had him by the shorts." Instead, he lined the canister up with the others, then gave a small shrug. "You kinda dropped this on us, Ma." He looked up and met her gaze, his own dead level.

Ellen Munroe held his eyes for a minute, then sighed and put the carafe on the coffeemaker element. "I know. And that wasn't very fair of us. But your father and I were afraid that some of you would try to talk us out of it. And there was no way Maria would accept any financial help from us." She looked up at him, a mixture of anxiety and concern in her eyes. "It was just awful when we got down there, Mitchell," she said, an odd catch in her voice as she explained. "They were absolutely destitute. Pedro's lengthy illness had used up whatever financial resources they had. And Maria had lost her job—you know, with that retired American couple she'd been with for the past few years. Anyway, they'd let her go because she missed work when she had to stay home and look after him."

Her face etched with the disturbing recollection, Ellen Munroe folded her arms and leaned back against the sink. She gave a small shrug. "So to put food on the table before he died, she and the boys had to take turns working in the chrysanthemum fields. They made nothing—barely subsistence wages. And by the time Pedro passed away, the Americans had moved to Costa Rica, and the area was so depressed there just wasn't anything else for her. So she's been working in the fields ever since."

Her arms still folded, his mother looked down and absently straightened the fringe on the mat in front of the sink, an odd catch in her voice when she spoke. "It broke my heart. I don't know how she's managed."

Hugging herself as if chilled by the recollection, she looked up at Mitch again, maternal despair in her eyes. "Then Roberto confided to your father that they had been learning English since they were very little, because someday they were all going to come to Canada. He told your dad that after his father died, they got an old coffee can with a lid on it, and they started hoarding every peso they could spare—so they could come live in Canada someday. Well," she said, turning her palms up, "what could we do? Your father and I agreed that we just couldn't leave them there like that. So we told them we'd bring them back with us, and everyone could get jobs and pay us back later."

Not wanting to put any of that information under an emotional microscope, Mitch shifted, bracing his hand against the corner of the fridge. His tone intended to mollify, he said, "Ma, this is between you and Dad. You're not accountable to any one of us. If the two of you decided to bring them home with you, then that's entirely your business. None of us have a say in that kind of decision. And I, for one, am going to keep my nose out of it."

Scrutinizing him with an intent look, Ellen Munroe finally spoke. "There is a difference between keeping your nose out of it and simply not engaging, Mitch. Sometimes I'm not sure you know the difference. No man is an island, you know."

Recognizing the chorus of a very old, familiar song, Mitch dropped his hand and straightened, bristling at his mother. "I'm not getting on that damned old hobbyhorse, Mother. So I think it would be best if I just got the damned keys for my van and went home.''

Not at all upset by his show of annoyance, Ellen Munroe continued to study her son. She gave him that certain smile that irritated him to no end, then responded, her tone even and unperturbed. ''The keys are on the front hall table. But you might find it hard to drive,'' she said, with that same distracted smile, ''with your head so firmly stuck in the sand.''

Without giving her the satisfaction of a rebuttal, and without even saying goodbye to his nephews, Mitch retrieved his keys and coat, slammed the door behind him and stomped out to his truck.

Once shut up in his van, he let go a string of swear words that would have permanently traumatized his nephews. Damn it all to hell, she was doing it to him again. Why in hell couldn't they all just leave him alone, and let him live his life as he saw fit? He was getting tired of all their opinions.

Starting the engine and slamming the vehicle into gear, he swung the wheel, the rear end fishtailing wildly on the ice along the curb. He had no damned intention of driving as sedately as his brother.

Mitch was still steaming when he pulled onto the main thoroughfare. Man, sometimes they just didn't get it. They didn't understand that he had a mission. And his mission was to mind his own business, with the hope that everyone else, especially his family, would make it a mission to mind their own. He was well aware that at least a third of his kin thought he was some kind of wounded animal gone to ground, another third thought he had turned into some sort of weird recluse, while the rest were sure that all he cared about was his business.

But they were all wrong. Every single one of them. He was none of the above. He just liked his life the way it was. And he had no intention of changing the status quo. Why should he? He was perfectly content.

Okay. So he might be forty and alone. But he'd tried marriage once—fifteen long years ago—and had found out the hard way it didn't work for him. It had been great for the first couple of years, then everything had gone to hell in a hand basket. And by the middle of the third year, he and his very young wife were hissing and spitting at each other like two barnyard cats. After six months of that, she'd realized it was never going to work, and that she may as well save herself a whole lot of grief and bail out. It wasn't so much that they weren't suited, it was about a whole lot of other things. She'd discovered she needed a life, and he was so young and stupid, he hadn't known how to give her that. He had wanted it his way. And his way had been one bloody big disaster.

It had taken him a while—a while to get over the hurt, and an even longer while to get over the devastation—but he'd finally seen the light. And realized he'd been a rotten candidate for marriage right from the beginning. He was too damned independent and self-centered to make a marriage work—maybe because he was the eldest of six kids; maybe because he was just too much like his grandfather, wanting to run the whole show. And no one could have that kind of attitude in a marriage. So he was better off on his own. Besides, he wasn't the kind of thickheaded dolt that had to get KO'd twice to get the message.

Unfortunately, his entire family—well, maybe not the *entire* family; mostly his mother and three sisters—had made it their collective life's work to find someone who was desperate enough to take him on. They thought his life was miserable and empty. He thought his life was just fine.

God, he just wished he didn't take the damned bait every time. Like getting riled over his mother's crack about "no man is an island." They were always doing that to him, giving him little jabs. And worse yet, giving him those long, wet-eyed, sympathetic looks—the ones that said his life was pathetic, and he was pathetic. Damn it, one of these days he was going to have to learn to get a grip.

Flashes of red and blue wigwag lights in his side mirror yanked him back to reality, and he swore, then threw on his signal light and pulled over onto the shoulder. Great. A speeding ticket was just what he needed. He'd been driving in such a blind snit, it took him a minute to figure out where he was. And where he was was about two hundred meters from the off ramp that would have taken him to his garden center. Swearing again, he put on his hazard lights and reached over, opened the glove compartment, then rummaged around until he located the folder that held his registration and insurance pink slip. He had his window rolled down and the documents ready and waiting by the time the police officer approached his vehicle. The officer shone his light in the window, then took the folder and removed the slips of paper, handing the folder back to Mitch.

With that nonexpression that cops learned in the

police academy, he scanned the documentation. "This is a commercial vehicle?"

Mitch expelled a very weary sigh. "Yes it is. It belongs to my company."

"Could I see your driver's license, sir?"

Mitchell fished it out of his wallet and handed it to him, his whole day reduced to this—being interrogated by some kid half his age.

"You were in a very big hurry back there, sir."

Mitch glanced at the cop. He was probably a couple of years older than half Mitch's age. Maybe closer to twenty-five years old, taking his job so seriously that he probably hadn't smiled since they'd handed him his badge. Mitch had no idea what possessed him, but for some reason, he just had to ask. "Tell me, Officer. Does your mother ever tick you off?"

With a totally unexpected response, the young cop suddenly grinned, meeting Mitch's jaded gaze. "Yes, sir. She certainly does."

Mitch nodded and sighed, then stared ahead out the windshield. "There ought to be a law."

Still grinning, the cop handed everything back through the window. "Under those circumstances, I'll let you off with a warning this time, Mr. Munroe. But in the future," he said, his grin getting bigger, "you might want to walk home from your mother's."

Not quite believing he wasn't going to get slammed with a speeding ticket, Mitch took the driver's license, pink slip and registration and tossed it on his dash. Hell, maybe his day hadn't been so bad, after all. How many people had ever come face-to-face with a traffic cop who had a sense of humor? Genuine amusement relaxing the muscles in his face, he pulled a business

card from under the clip on his visor. Giving the kid
a lopsided grin, he handed it to him. "Tell you what.
Come see me on Mother's Day. We'll make your
mother a happy woman."

The kid took the card and stuck it in the inside
pocket of his winter jacket. "I don't think so, sir." He
gave Mitch another big grin. "Not unless I can make
her a grandmother before then."

Mitch returned his two-fingered salute, switched off
his hazard lights and put the truck in gear. Maybe he
didn't have it so bad, after all.

Chapter 2

February 25

Mitch hunched over his desk, the phone tucked between his shoulder and ear, a pencil in his hand, half a dozen spreadsheets laid out in front of him. A stack of garden catalogs and order forms teetered on the corner of his desk, and he shoved them over and straightened the pile, annoyance flickering through him. He was going to be so glad when all the distributors climbed into the communication age and started using the Internet.

Reaching his maximum-irritation flash point, he slammed down the phone and looked at his watch. Seventeen minutes on hold. The first time he'd tried, he'd just got bloody voice mail. And now this. It was enough to drive a guy to drink.

He stuck the pencil behind his ear and checked his watch. He wanted to take twenty minutes to go over the spreadsheets Jordan had printed off for him, but he also had to remember that he had to pick up his grandmother from the doctor's at three. And that was one appointment he absolutely had to make, because if he wasn't there waiting for her, Baba would simply get on the bus and go it on her own. Sometimes that old girl gave him strokes.

And he still hadn't had lunch. Which meant going out for something to eat, because there wasn't a damned thing in his fridge upstairs. Nothing. Nil. Nada.

Mitch gave his office an automatic perusal and grimaced, deciding he had to get a grip on this mess. One corner was filled with dead or dying plants—a little ongoing practical joke from his staff. His bookshelves were a disorganized mess, and every drawer of his file cabinet was hanging open. But at least all the mail was caught up and the bills had been paid. He wasn't sure how he'd ever managed without Jordan.

He checked his watch again and swore under his breath. Hell, where had the morning gone?

"Oh, Lord. I hope all that muttering doesn't bode badly. Are you going to throw me off the bridge or just yell at me? You sound mean enough to eat little children."

Mitch looked up, a small smile appearing when he saw the pose his sister had struck in his doorway. Cora was part of a matched set. Although she and her twin, Caroline, were identical in looks, their dispositions were as different as night and day. Caroline was calm and logical and loved to be entertained. Cora, on the other hand, was quick and sharp-witted, as flamboyant as a thirties movie star, and loved to entertain. When they were kids, she'd constantly played to Caroline's spectator mode and ready sense of humor. But as different as they were, they were still as thick as thieves. Like her younger twin, Cora was tall, with the dark, blue-eyed Irish looks of their grandfather. She also had the clothes sense of a fashion designer. Swathed in a black coat and a dramatic black-and-white scarf and topped off in something that looked like a black Cossack hat, she looked as if she had stepped out of a fashion magazine. Only right then she was doing her *Perils of Pauline* routine, standing with her back flattened against the door frame, her arm extended, her palm out, as if she were expecting him to tie her to a train trestle. Sometimes his siblings' inferences that he was a grump amused him, sometimes they didn't. Today, she amused him.

Folding his arms, he leaned back in his chair and propped his feet up on the overflowing metal wastebasket. He gave her a nasty grin. "So what are you doing so far from the office? Or are you just out chasing ambulances?"

Cora was a lawyer, a very successful corporate one, and he doubted if she'd settled a single injury claim in her entire career. But he took every opportunity to needle her, especially since she was the worst offender as a marriage broker, constantly trying to palm him off on any single woman under the age of seventy who had breath left in her.

She dropped her hand, lifted her chin and gave him an imperious look down the length of her elegant nose.

"Very funny, Fertilizer Man." As if shedding a skin, she dropped her phony persona and entered the room. She tossed her pricey handbag in an empty chair, then flopped down in the other chair facing him. As she looked across at him, her expression turned serious. "We've got a problem, Mitch."

He didn't like the sound of that one bit. Especially the "we" part. And especially when he didn't have a clue what she was talking about. Somehow he managed to keep from physically recoiling. "And what's that?"

She pulled off her leather gloves, then met his gaze again. "Do you have any idea what's going on with the Rodriguezes?"

Feeling particularly smug and satisfied with himself for not having a single clue about what was going on with any of them, he rocked back in his chair, folded his arms and shook his head. "Nope."

"Well, you'd better."

Mitch didn't like the sound of that, either, but he also knew there wasn't a hope in hell that she would read his silence for what it was—a mind-your-own-business reticence. And he was right.

Cora continued. "Mom and Dad's motives might have been sterling silver, but their judgement wasn't." She shook her head as if rehashing something in her mind; then she leaned back in her chair and sighed, her expression lawyerlike. "They thought getting them here was the big hurdle. And yes, they pulled some very major strings to get their Mexican passports on such short notice, especially when Grandfather probably didn't even have so much as a baptismal certificate as proof of nationality. And they did use their heads and get the passports stamped for ninety days. But that's as far as they went. It would have been better if they'd arranged for six-month visitor visas, but that still wouldn't have made much difference.''

She laid out her gloves on her knee, her expression preoccupied as she carefully arranged them finger to finger. Finally she met Mitch's gaze. ''Dad thinks that the hard part is over. He's certain that all we have to do now is line up a job for Maria, and with Mom and him sponsoring them, the entire family can go ahead and apply for landed immigrant status. And he's convinced that they're going to be able to stay. But that's not how it works. They're in for a rude awakening.''

Mitch frowned. ''What do you mean by a rude awakening?''

Looking truly worried, Cora shrugged, her expression somber. ''They can't apply for landed immigrant status from within Canada, Mitch, not unless they claim refugee status. Which they can't. They aren't refugees. And let's face it, they don't exactly have the skills or the financial wherewithal to score high with Immigration's formula.''

She closed her eyes and rubbed a spot between her brows, as if she were acquiring a family-induced headache. Then she exhaled a long breath and looked at her brother. ''Mom and Dad screwed up, and I don't know how to tell them. The Rodriguezes aren't going to be able to stay, Mitch. And when I found out this morning what Mom and Dad had intended, I just about fell through the floor. I thought they were here for a lengthy visit—that's all. I didn't know they were here for good. I just didn't know what to say.''

Mitch considered his sister, his own expression sober. He knew where this was heading, and he released a weary sigh. He guessed it wouldn't kill him. "Do you want me to talk to them?"

Clearly troubled, Cora gave a little shrug. "It's not so much telling Mom and Dad," she said, her voice uneven. "It's having to tell those boys. They're such great kids, and this is a dream come true for them. All their lives they've dreamed about coming to Canada." She made a helpless gesture with her hands. "Did Mom and Dad tell you about their coffee can bank?"

Mitch nodded, and she looked even more pathetic. "God, I don't want to be the one to tell them they don't stand a chance."

She looked at him, her eyes so full of woe he couldn't stand it. Leaning forward on his elbows to break visual contact, Mitch began fiddling with some loose paper clips on his desk. He understood where she was coming from, he really did. He could remember when she'd been about three and totally heartbroken when the head had come off her pink fluffy bunny. She had mourned for days, and this was in a whole different category. This was about very real people in a very real plight.

His voice was gruff when he finally answered. "You shouldn't have to tell them, Cora. And we both know what Dad is like. It'll be best if I tell 'em."

Managing a watery smile, she blotted her eyes with the inside cuff of her glove. "Yeah, well... But to be absolutely frank here, Dad wouldn't listen to a word I was saying, anyway. He still thinks I'm six years old and playing with dolls. However, he does listen to you." She drew in a deep breath, as if to settle her emotions. After a moment, she got up. "I'll make you a swap. I know you said you'd pick Baba up today, but I can do that. I'll call her and tell her.'' She gave him a wry smile. ''I know it's a pretty unfair swap, big brother. But right now, it's the best I can do.''

He looked up at her, his own smile a little off-kilter. ''You just remember that you owe me one, little sister. And don't you forget about this when I call you on it.''

She chuckled and picked up her bag. ''That'll depend on how good my memory is at the time, Mitchell, darling. It will all depend.''

After Cora left, he considered phoning Immigration just to double-check the regulations, but then decided against it. He really, truly did not want to know. Accurate information was not a plus in this family. And besides, Cora had given him the information, and she should know. All he was going to be was the messenger boy. This was one family upheaval he wasn't getting embroiled in. No damned way. Not a chance.

It was just going on five when he finally cleared the decks to a point where he could leave with a halfway clear conscience. The garden center stayed open until nine every night, with the exception of Saturdays and Sundays during the winter months. But his main man, which happened to be a woman, was working tonight and she could handle closing. Which left him free to go handle his parents. He almost felt as if he should suit up for battle.

Ice fog was hanging in the air, creating misty halos around the streetlights and casting the sky in a faint pink hue. By the time he pulled up in front of his parents' house, hoarfrost was beginning to collect on the shrubs and trees, creating a sparkling coating on the snow. By morning, there would be a thick layer on everything, and it would be beautiful along the creek that ran through one corner of his property.

His mother had twinkly little white lights strung through the shrubs in front of the house and through the trees in the backyard. It wasn't a Christmas thing. It was an all-season thing for her, and her grandchildren loved it. Grandma's fairy lights. He kind of liked them himself. Especially now, with the dusting of frost just settling in.

Mitch parked on the freshly shoveled driveway, then got out of his Jeep and reached into the back seat, lifting a plastic-and-paper-shrouded plant from the floor. It was a gardenia plant covered in buds, and it would be covered in white blossoms in the next couple of days. His mother would love it.

He went up the front walk, did a rat-tat-tat on the door and entered, the crisp cold air sweeping in with him. Closing the door behind him, he slipped out of his boots and unsnapped the buttons on his jacket.

His mother stuck her head around the corner. "Mitchell! What a nice surprise. And what perfect timing. We're just about to sit down to dinner. Can you stay?"

Dinner? His parents never ate dinner this early. He glanced at the old grandmother clock sitting on the mantel of the fireplace. It wasn't early. It was nearly half past six. Hell, where had the past hour gone? He'd been losing time the whole damned day.

Giving his head a shake, he straightened and handed his mother the plant. He gave her a warped grin. "It depends what you're having. If it's one of those rotten casseroles you used to try and feed us when we were kids, count me out.''

She smacked his shoulder. ''God, you are awful.'' She tried to peek in through the wraps on the plant. ''And what do we have here?''

His mother might be in her midsixties, but she looked and acted half her age. He responded to her question, his tone dry. ''It's a casserole plant.'' Stripping off his coat, he hung it on the doorknob, then headed toward the kitchen. Before he made a commitment about dinner, he was going to check out what was happening on the stove.

He entered the large country kitchen, bracing himself for a crowd around the table. But there were only three places set. Maria was at the work island, slicing tomatoes. She had on a set of deep purple sweats he recognized as his mother's—sweats that she filled out far more than his mother did—and she had her black hair tied back and bound with a scarlet ribbon. The bold colors suited her. She looked up as he entered, then gave him a careful smile. ''Good evening, Mitchell.''

Dragging up an ill-used set of manners, Mitch returned a carbon copy of her careful smile. ''Hello, Maria. How did your first week in Canada go?''

She gave a little shrug, but there was a glimmer of amusement in her eyes. ''Your snow is very cold.''

He nodded and glanced at the table again, then pointedly looked at his mother. Intercepting his silent query, Ellen Munroe set the plant next to the sink on the opposite end of the work island, then began unwrapping it. ''Murphy had extra tickets to the hockey game, so he took the boys and Grandfather Rodriguez. He figured they'd get a kick out of it.''

Out of the corner of his eye, Mitch saw Maria frown and mouth the phrase. He experienced a twist of humor. Folding his arms, he leaned back against the counter and explained. ''To get a kick out of something is an idiom, Maria.''

Her eyes lit up and her mouth got round with understanding. He gave her a small smile. ''It means they will likely enjoy themselves, have a good time.''

''Ah,'' she said, getting the picture, the twinkle once again appearing in her eyes. ''The same as to have a blast?''

He chuckled and nodded. ''Exactly.''

''Yes,'' she said, her tone knowing as she returned to her task. ''To get a kick.'' Just from her expression, he knew she was imprinting the phrase and the meaning on her mind.

Mitch glanced at his mother. ''Where's Dad? How come he didn't go to the hockey game?''

''It's his poker night.'' His mother tore the last layer of protective paper, stripping it away. ''Oh, Mitchell. It's beautiful. Just what I need for the center of the table.'' She tipped it so Maria could see. ''Isn't it beautiful, Maria?''

Maria nodded, then frowned, as if she were trying to mentally retrieve something. Then she suddenly smiled the first full smile Mitch had seen from her, revealing a set of perfect teeth and matching dimples. ''Gardenias,'' she said, obviously pleased with herself for remembering the correct English word. ''They are beautiful. And,'' she said, making a very Latin gesture of approval with her hands, ''they smell like heaven.''

She turned the full force of her smile on Mitch, and he experienced a rush of electricity that shot all the way down to his toes. For one awful minute, he thought he was going to break out in a sweat. And he didn't like the feeling at all. Abruptly straightening, he turned toward the hallway. "I think I'll go check on what Dad's up to," he said, his tone slightly choked. Damn. A buzz like that—maybe he was coming down with something.

He finally found his father in the attached garage, puttering with something on his workbench. His father's hair had gone from salt-and-pepper gray to totally white in the past couple of years, and there was a hint of a stoop appearing in his shoulders. But what had changed the most were his hands. Somewhere along the line, they had become an old man's hands. Mitchell didn't like to think about it.

Patrick Munroe glanced up when his son opened the door, tipping his head down so he could see over the top of his half glasses. "Good God. Look what crawled out of the woodwork. And to what do we owe this pleasure?"

His father was one of the group of kith and kin who thought Mitchell had turned into some sort of bad-tempered hermit. Sometimes Mitch would have liked to take all his kith and kin and stuff them down a very large hole. "Very funny, Dad."

His dad nodded, a twinkle appearing in his eyes. "I am, aren't I?"

He waved Mitch over to a paint-spattered stool. "Take a load off."

It was a fishing reel his father had apart, and Mitch stuffed his hands in his pockets as he watched him reset a tiny screw. Figuring now was as good a time as any, he put on his messenger's hat. "Cora came to see me today."

"Hmm? And what did your sister want? Or has she decided to sue you?" His father chuckled at his own joke; Mitch was only minimally amused. He picked up a large washer off the bench, then rolled it over and between his fingers in a magician's trick he'd learned when he was about nine years old. Knowing he was stalling, he palmed the washer and began tossing it in his hand. "She had some bad news, and she didn't know how to tell you."

Still gripping the screwdriver, Patrick Munroe again looked at his son over the top of his glasses. "And what bad news would that be?"

Drawing a deep breath to prepare himself, Mitch stopped fiddling with the washer and met his father's level gaze. "She said you aren't going to be able to apply for landed immigrant status for the Rodriguezes from here—that they'll have to apply from outside the country." Seeing his father was about to butt in, he held up his hand, successfully overriding the interruption. "And she also has concerns about them meeting immigration requirements. She doesn't think they'll qualify."

His father's salt-and-pepper eyebrows shot up, and annoyance glittered in his eyes. "That's a load of hogwash. Your mother and I are going to sponsor them, so why should Immigration give a damn one way or another?"

Making sure his tone remained absolutely neutral, Mitch forced the muscles in his jaw to relax before he responded. "I'm only telling you what Cora said, Dad.

She's pretty worried about it. She figured you and Mom should know what you're up against.'' Mitchell tossed the washer into a container of nuts and bolts at the back of the workbench, then stuck his hands in his pockets. ''She thought it might be a good idea if you lined up an immigration lawyer.''

His dad snorted and slammed the screwdriver down. ''Well, that's just bloody ridiculous.''

''What's bloody ridiculous, dear?''

Both men looked up. Ellen Munroe had her head poked around the partially open door. His father repeated what Mitchell had told him, word for word, bristling with annoyance.

Ellen listened, then waved it all off. ''Cora just got her wires crossed. She doesn't practice immigration law.'' She motioned them in. ''Now come for dinner.''

Mitch experienced some annoyance of his own. Damn it, why couldn't his old man just listen for once? He wanted to argue with his father, but he never got the chance. Patrick bustled off, leaving Mitch standing there, his irritation making his jaws ache. The exchange reminded Mitch of countless go-arounds they'd had when he'd been a kid still living at home, when his father would just refuse to listen. No wonder Cora didn't want to confront him—he probably would have patted her on the head and sent her out to play. Lord, his father could be the most mule-minded, unreasonable, thickheaded man on the face of the entire earth.

Swearing under his breath, Mitch stomped into the house after them. To hell with supper. He had better things to do with his time. Damned straight, he did.

But the look on Maria Rodriguez's face when he

reached the kitchen had him ditching that idea. It was as if she knew something was going on, and she had that worried, pinched expression again. Hell. It wasn't her fault that his parents were such dingbats. So he stayed. He ate. He even managed small talk. And he let on as if nothing was wrong.

But it was a bloody wonder he didn't get pulled over on the way home again. If parents thought their kids were aggravating—by God, he'd match his parents up against a roomful of kids any day.

There was a truckload of potting soil waiting for him to move when he arrived back at the center, and nothing burned off that kind of aggravation like some darned hard work. By nine that night, Mitch had pretty much cooled off. By midnight, he could even see a tiny spark of humor in it. But one thing for sure, that was the last time he was going to get tangled up in the Rodriguez affair.

It was brother Murphy who showed up at his office door two days later. His appearance wasn't half as dramatic as Cora's, but it was pretty darned obvious his brother was up to no good. He had that level-eyed, gunslinger expression on his face, and that look always spelled trouble.

When Murphy came in and shut the door, Mitch watched him with a jaundiced look, wondering what his life would have been like as an only child.

Murphy tossed his hat in a chair and sprawled in the same chair Cora had.

Folding his arms across his chest, Mitch rolled his own chair back from the desk.

Murphy gave him an ingratiating grin. "So how are things, bro?"

His eyes narrow and his jaw fixed, Mitch stared back at him. "Don't 'bro' me. And the answer is no. Absolutely not. Not a chance."

Murphy at least had the decency to look guilty. "What?"

His eyes still narrowed, Mitch shook his head. "Whatever it is, I'm not doing it. I said no."

Murphy grinned again, tipping his head to one side as he considered his brother. "No, huh?"

"That's right. No."

Murphy studied him a moment longer, that same annoying grin on his face; then he reached back and opened the door and called for his big gun. "Jordan, honey. Would you come in here?"

Jordan appeared at the doorway, her hair pulled back in a severely neat style, a set of pearl studs in her ears. Looking very cool and efficient in a chocolate-colored power suit that totally camouflaged her round little belly, she grinned, ruining the entire cool, elegant effect. "Hi, Mitch. How's it going?"

Mitch felt defeat set in.

His gaze still fixed on Mitch, Murphy spoke to her, his voice getting that odd huskiness in it. "Tell him why we're here, darlin'."

Jordan's expression changed, and it was clearly obvious, even to Mitch, that whatever she was going to tell him truly upset her. For one awful moment, Mitch thought she might actually cry. And Jordan wasn't the type to cry over just anything. She wrung her hands together and a dark, anxious look appeared in her eyes. Her attention riveted on him, she started to speak, her

tone distraught. "We went over to your mom and
dad's last night, and Maria caught me alone in the
kitchen. She looked so worried, and she wanted to
know what she had to do so she could get a job."

Her voice got a catch in it, and she glanced at her
husband, who nodded, silently prompting her to continue. Jordan looked back at Mitch, an urgent expression on her face. "She has nothing, Mitch. And she's
worried sick about money. And I know you usually
start hiring casual labor fairly soon."

She made a nervous gesture with her hands, then
started talking very fast, as if she wasn't going to give
him a chance to interrupt. "I know…I know you can't
claim her as an employee, and I know it's illegal to
hire her. But Murphy and I will pay part of her wage,
if you can just give her a legitimate job—one that she
knows is legitimate. We tried to come up with something ourselves, but we've got nothing. There's not a
thing for her to do at Murphy's construction company,
especially this time of year. And I don't have anything
for her to do, except housework, and we were both
pretty sure she would see that as token."

Jordan stopped for a breath, her face still tight with
worry. "And we thought it wasn't all that wise to
approach anyone else—that it would be best if we kept
it just among the three of us. We really did try to figure
out something, but we kept coming back to the greenhouse. And it's not as if she's totally inexperienced.
She *has* worked in the chrysanthemum fields, and
Mom Munroe says she's very creative."

Jordan pressed her hands together, looking at him
with that hopeful anxiety of hers, beseeching him,
pleading with him with those great big gray eyes. "I

just can't imagine being in her shoes, Mitch—in a strange country without a cent to my name. It would be so terrifying.''

His own expression sober, Murphy rose and went over to his wife, then wrapped his arm around her shoulders and pulled her against him. He kissed her hair, then looked at his brother.

Mitch had never seen anyone like Murphy, somebody who could manage to have two completely different expressions on his face at the same time. Like now. One expression was all soft and tender, full of care and concern for his wife. Then there was the other expression, the one that was a smug ''gotcha'' look reserved entirely for his brother. Mitch stared back, knowing he'd been toast the minute Jordan opened her mouth. He wondered, if he ran away to Mexico, if *he* could get a job in the chrysanthemum fields.

Finally he rolled his eyes toward the ceiling, heaved a sigh and capitulated. ''All right. I can come up with something. I'll go talk to her tonight.'' He pointed his finger at his brother. ''But this is it, Murphy. I'm not getting dragged into this any further.''

Murphy grinned and measured a distance with his thumb and forefinger. ''Not an inch.'' Jordan came over and squeezed his shoulder, her expression filled with gratitude—the kind of gratitude that came straight from the heart. ''Thank you, Mitchell,'' she whispered softly, then bent down and kissed him on the cheek. ''I knew we could count on you.''

It was as if this reluctant agreement metamorphosed into a large, bulbous, ghostlike shape that hunkered down on the corner of his desk, determined to remind him second by second for the rest of the day what he'd agreed to do. Finally he escaped and headed into the garden center and set about creating havoc for his staff.

Mitch managed to find busywork until well into the evening, and he only stopped then because he was forced to head out to get something to eat.

It was nearly eight o'clock when he once again pulled up in front of his parents' house. This time the fairy lights in the shrubs annoyed him to no end. God, it was time she gave that silly fairy thing a rest.

He didn't knock; he just let himself in. They were all likely in the family room downstairs, watching TV, and they wouldn't hear him anyway. And the damned doorbell had broken at least five months ago, and his mother had decided not to get it fixed. She insisted she quite liked not having one.

The living room was empty, but there was a light in the kitchen. Mitch headed toward it, expecting to find his mother.

Only one light was on in the big room—the large oblong stained-glass fixture hanging over the round table. The rest of the room was boxed in shadows. But it wasn't his mother seated at the kitchen table. It was Maria, with several books stacked up before her.

She had on a red dress with a full skirt, the color nearly faded to pink, and her thick hair was pulled back in a neat French braid. The overhead light caught the glossy shine of her coal-black hair, the angle casting shadows on her high cheekbones and accentuating her exceptionally long eyelashes. The potted gardenia, now covered in blossoms, was positioned to her left, its waxy leaves also reflecting the light. It was the kind of image that begged to be photographed—dark shadows, and a beautiful woman within a soft circle of light, with the flowers there beside her.

Totally engrossed in whatever she was reading, she was sitting with her head propped on one hand as she absently twirled a loose tendril of hair around her finger. She was so intent, he was pretty sure she hadn't even heard him come in.

Great. Now he was going to scare her to death.

He cleared his throat, and she came out of the chair a good two feet as she jerked around to face him. Clamping her hand against her chest, she blew out a long breath, giving a weak laugh. "Ah. Mitchell. You walk on little feet."

The "little feet" comment almost made him smile. Little feet—not hardly. But he got the drift of what she meant. Maybe because his appearance had so clearly startled her, or maybe because of the comment about little feet, his earlier reticence eased off. And for some reason he didn't even bother to try to fathom, he found himself strangely at ease.

"Sorry," he said, approaching the table. "I didn't mean to startle you." Sticking his hands in his pockets, he glanced down at the books scattered on the table. The manual in front of her was actually an English vocabulary workbook. She was working on the *S*s. The other books stacked up by her elbow were two English-as-a-second-language textbooks, a Spanish-English dictionary, and a copy of an old Dickens classic.

Taking his hand out of his pocket, he flipped open the cover of the novel. "I remember this book. One

winter when we all had measles and chicken pox,
Mom read us a chapter every night.''

Maria spoke, her tone wry. ''You must have been
very...'' she glanced at the book, then continued
''...very stalwart children.'' She looked at him in con-
firmation. ''Stalwart, yes?''

He nodded, and she gave him a self-satisfied smile,
pleased with herself for using a new word correctly.

Keeping his own expression restrained, he looked
back down at the book and flipped through a few
pages, then glanced back at her, his curiosity piqued.
''Why do you think we were stalwart?''

She gave a sheepish little grimace. ''In places it is
very...tedious.''

Mitch laughed. He could remember being bored
right out of his mind during the endless reading of the
book. But he'd always thought it was because they'd
been cooped up for days with measles. And just when
they were all about ready to go back to school, they
had all come down with chicken pox. He often wondered how his mother had survived having six sick,
cranky kids all cooped up together.

He was still grinning as he met Maria's gaze. ''It
was pretty boring, all right.'' Realizing what he had
said, he made a modification. ''Very boring.''

She slanted a look up at him. ''I understand the
connotation of 'pretty,' Mitchell. Although it does not
make much sense.''

He chuckled and flipped through a few more pages.
''I imagine there's a whole lot that doesn't make much
sense.''

Knowing he was using the novel as a stall tactic—
and that he was allowing himself to get sidetracked—

he pulled out a chair and sat down. Man, he wished he hadn't let himself get talked into this. He was going to regret it; he knew damned well he was.

Suddenly wishing he had chosen a chair farther away from her, he carefully squared up the pile of books; then he exhaled sharply and looked at her. "You know that I own a garden center?"

Her gaze fixed on him, she slowly nodded.

She had quit playing with that one tendril of hair, and it curled along the side of her neck. The skin was so soft there, and delicate. It was such a damned distraction, the way that curl brushed against her skin, and it was all Mitch could do to keep from tucking it back into the braid. It was only hair, for God's sake.

Deliberately hooking his thumb in the belt loop on his jeans, Mitch held her gaze for a second. Then he looked away and very precisely readjusted the alignment of the books, a funny sensation unfurling in his chest. For some reason he did not want to lie to this woman. Needing to fortify himself, he took a breath. "I'm making some changes in display areas, and I'm going to need some extra help for the next little while." It was all he could do to look at her. "I was wondering if you'd be interested in a job."

Her expression went very still, and he could see the wild flutter of the pulse in her neck. As if fearful to believe her good luck, she swallowed hard and clasped her hands between her thighs, her solemn eyes as round as saucers. She stared at him, then finally spoke, her tone an awed whisper. "You can do this? You can give me a job without proper papers?"

Mitch didn't know why, but this lie was easier to tell. "I can hire casual labor." Which was true—he just wasn't supposed to hire casual laborers who didn't possess a Canadian social insurance number. Or in her case, a work visa.

She clutched her hands together in her lap, the pulse in her neck still going a mile a minute. "Yes. I would be very interested."

Unable to hold her gaze any longer, he ran his thumb along the spine of the top text. He told her the hours he wanted her to work and what her hourly wage would be, but she didn't even give him time to finish.

"No, Mitchell," she interjected, horror in her voice. "That is too much. I cannot accept such an amount."

He lifted his gaze and looked at her, the muscles in his face going unnaturally stiff. "That's my going rate, Maria," he said. "It's what I pay all my part-time help."

"But it is too much."

Her insistence that it was too much annoyed him. Okay, so his rate was well above minimum wage, but he got good staff who stayed. He managed a tight smile. "Well, this is the first time I've had that complaint."

As if it suddenly dawned on her that she might have offended him, she reached out and touched his arm, her expression wide-eyed with alarm. "You misunderstand, Mitchell. I am not complaining. I would take the job for fewer money."

Without thinking, he corrected her. "For less money."

She made a grimace at her mistake, but there was also a glint of mischief in her eyes. "Yes. That is correct, Mitchell. I will take the job for *less* money."

There was something about watching someone's

mind work that had always fascinated him, and watching hers was more fascinating than most. He leaned back in his chair, determined to win this round. "No. You won't take it for *less* money, Maria. That is what this job pays."

She watched him with an unblinking stare, assessing how far she could push him. But she obviously understood the idiom "between a rock and hard place," because she finally sighed and relented. However, she did have to have the last word, even if it was muttered for her own benefit. "But it is still too much."

Not about to let her get away with that, he sent her a long look. "Give it a rest, Rodriguez. If you want the job, you can start at nine tomorrow morning."

She glared at him, and he could tell she was itching to fight over it, but she lifted her chin and gave him a level look. "I will give it a rest, *Mitchell*. For now."

He wanted to grin at her cheekiness, but he didn't. He had a feeling he was going to have to fight hard to hold his ground, or she'd simply run right over him. Realizing what he had just gotten himself into, he felt his own expression turn glum. Yeah, he was going to have to hold his ground with this one all right. If he didn't go to jail first.

Chapter 3

The following morning dawned with a dismal sky, and Mitchell put off unlocking the front doors of Fairhaven Nurseries for as long as he could.

There were two reasons why he wasn't all that enthused. First of all, it had snowed heavily all night, and the parking lot was now one big snowdrift. Which meant he had literally tons of snow to remove before customers started arriving, or there would be vehicles stuck all over the place.

And secondly, he dreaded having to tell Doris, his "main man," what he had done, hiring Maria. Doris would give him that long look and that smug smile, as if she knew something about him that he didn't know. Then she would pat him on the cheek as if he were some abandoned puppy she'd found at the dog pound. Sometimes Doris gave him one hell of a headache. Probably because she refused to call a bleeding heart a bleeding heart. No. She had to call it a *dicentra spectabilis*. Half the time he didn't know what in hell she was talking about.

Shrugging into his jacket, he did up the snaps and pulled up the collar, then picked up a pair of gloves. Grabbing a shovel off the rack by the exit, he headed outside. If he could get the concrete apron in front of the doors cleared before everybody arrived, it would keep ice to a minimum. And it would also save a whole lot of mopping up later on.

The day was cloudy and overcast and the air was crisp and clear, and the cold air hitting his lungs was better than a shot of pure oxygen. It was so still out that nothing moved, and his breath hung in the air.

Resting his hand on the handle of the shovel, he studied his domain. If he did say so himself, he had done some very creative landscaping around the parking lot—clumps of evergreens and birch intermingled with clusters of various shrubs, with more flowering shrubs scattered among the maple and ash trees. And in the summer, the surrounding beds were filled to bursting with a vibrant mix of annuals and perennials, and the vine-covered arbors were vivid with blossoms. It was truly a spectacular show in the summer and fall, and his customers spent as much time outside in the gardens as they did inside shopping. But now, with drifts covering everything, the only real color against the white was the red bark of the dogwood and dark green of the fir trees.

A clump of snow slid from the branches of a huge old spruce, marring the satin smoothness of the drift below, the soft plop startling a wild rabbit that had taken shelter beneath the screen of branches. He watched the animal hop away and disappear in a warren of snow-covered shrubs.

He loved it when it was quiet and perfectly still like this—without a sound except the chatter of a flock of chickadees and the muffled hum of traffic in the distance. This was the kind of silence that filled him up. But then, he liked winter, always had, probably because his life was so damned hectic during the summer months. A day like today was as good as a week's holiday.

Making a mental note that the bird feeders needed refilling, he began shoveling the heavy snow. As soon as Doris got here to handle everything inside, he'd get the Bobcat out and start clearing the parking lot. Which would give him a perfect excuse to stay outdoors. Which also meant he could avoid those long, knowing looks of Doris's.

He had already cleared the apron and was using a broom to knock the snow off the row of double-tray shopping carts when a blue four-wheel-drive truck roared into the lot, spewing chewed-up snow as it slid around a corner. Folding down his collar, which was now stiff with frost, he watched as the vehicle pulled into a clear space by one of the storage sheds. A tall woman with gray hair got out, a bright red-and-green scarf wound around her neck. "Good morning, Boss. I see you've been busy working up to your first heart attack."

Resting his hand on the broom handle, he watched her. "Very funny, Doris."

She grinned at him as she crossed the parking lot, wading through thigh-high drifts in spots. Reaching him and the clear entryway, she stamped her feet and brushed the snow off her slacks. "So. I suppose this big dump is going to be your excuse to bugger off and leave us with that big inventory shuffle you decided you just had to have."

He jammed the broom handle beside the shovel in the snow pile. Hell, he had been so busy thinking about what he'd gotten himself into by hiring Maria Rodriguez, he had totally forgotten the big rearrangement job. And he hadn't even drafted up a plan. Great. There wasn't a chance in hell Doris Becker would ever let him live that down.

But he knew from experience that his best defense with her was a strong offense. Yanking off a glove, he pulled a red bandanna out of his pocket and wiped his nose. Finally he met her gaze. "We need to have a talk," he said, keeping his expression neutral. He stuffed the bandanna back in his pocket, then rested his hand on the handle of the shovel. "I'm sure you've heard about my parents bringing a family back with them from Mexico."

Doris watched him, a serious expression on her face. "You mean Maria and her family."

Mitch nodded, then glanced across his property. He thought about the pros and cons of telling her the whole story, of turning her into an accomplice in something that was not exactly legal; then he decided to go for broke. She deserved to know exactly what was going on. Besides, Doris had never once let him down during the twelve years she had worked for him. Not once.

Expelling his breath in a heavy sigh, he pulled the shovel out of the drift and began began making crosshatches in the snow with its blade. "Apparently she's in pretty dire straits financially, and Cora figures they're in big trouble as far as applying for landed status goes. So Murphy and Jordan came up with a plan." He looked at Doris, his expression serious. "She's going to be working here. But we have to do it on the QT. If Immigration was ever to find out she was working without a visa, they'd bounce her out of the country in about ten seconds flat."

Doris considered her boss. "Not to mention what they would do to you."

He shrugged off her comment and stared out across the expanse of white. She didn't say anything for a moment; then she spoke. "So. As far as everybody else is concerned, she's just helping out. That's the story we're going with, right?"

He nodded. "Yeah. That's about it. But I want you to treat her like staff. She has to feel as if she's a viable part of the work force—as Jordan put it, we don't want it to appear token. And I don't want her thinking this is charity. Jordan is going to work out an advance for her, so if she mentions it, let on that's a common practice."

He pulled the shovel toward him, then jammed it back into the pile of snow. "I'm going to need you to somehow get the tactful point across that she's not to discuss wages. When I talked to her about it last night, she was pretty adamant that I was offering her too much, so she might bring it up here. And I'd rather no one else knew she was getting paid. I don't want anyone else dragged into this if we can help it, especially if any government hounds start sniffing around."

When he turned his attention back to her, Doris was

watching him with an intent look, her arms folded, her head tipped to one side. "And of course, you don't want her to know you could get your ass in a sling for paying her, right? Or that this is a make-work project?"

He scowled at his manager. "Don't start with that crap, all right?" he snapped. "And it's not a make-work project. We've needed to overhaul the setup for the past two years, and we just never got around to it. So she's going to be working, all right. Don't kid yourself. And if you want to start handing out bouquets, give them to Jordan. It was her idea."

Doris smiled that aggravating smile of hers. "Yeah. Right." Then she patted him on the cheek, just like he knew she would, and turned toward the door. "Rest assured, Bossman. I will have the wisdom of Solomon, the silence of the Sphinx and the vigilance of a junk-yard dog." She grinned at him over her shoulder. "But I'm going to let you handle the first introductory steps, my man." She lifted her chin toward the access road. "Looks like your new employee is about to be delivered."

Feeling as if his manager had just dropped a rock in his belly, Mitch glanced toward the road. A half-ton truck with Munroe Construction emblazoned on the door was fishtailing around the curve, snow flying in its wake. Mitch jammed his hands on his hips and looked at the sky. God, sometimes his brother was such an idiot. Trust him to scare her half to death driving like that, especially on her first day of work in a strange country.

He could see Murphy grinning as he pulled up in front of Mitch. Mitch wanted to smack him. Maria got out, all bundled up in a long navy coat that had once been Jordan's and a white woolly hat and scarf. She had a smile as big as Texas on her face and her eyes were bright with delight. "This is so…" she hesitated, searching through her word bank "…so amazing. And the drive to get here was most exciting. I have never seen snow like this. It is beautiful, is it not, Mitchell?"

Grinning broadly, Murphy tipped his head so he could eyeball his brother through the open door. "She's a crazy woman, bro. Thinks all this is great fun."

She made a very Latin, dismissive gesture at Murphy, flashing her dimples. "It is great fun." Then she sent him a charming smile. "Thank you for driving me this morning, Murphy. It was good of you to do that. But tomorrow I will take the bus."

Mitch gave a wry half smile. "It wasn't good of him, Maria. He thought it would be great fun to scare you half to death."

She shot Mitchell an appreciative look, then waggled her finger at Murphy. "Now I know the truth about you, Mr. Munroe. I do not scare that easily. And I will not be so trusting next time."

Murphy grinned at the two standing outside, flipping Mitch a two-finger salute. "I'll see you guys later."

Shutting the truck door and stepping back, Maria watched as Murphy roared out of the parking lot. Then she turned and looked at Mitchell, her expression almost shy as she gave him a little grimace. "I am not late, no?"

He shook his head, wishing he hadn't gotten talked into this. "No. You're early in fact."

Mitch pulled off his other glove and went toward the door, stamping the snow from his feet as it slid open. "Come in. I'll introduce you to Doris. She manages the garden center for me."

Maria mimicked his movements to a T, carefully stamping the snow off her feet as well. For some reason, her actions amused him. He'd seen his nephew J.J. do the exact same thing, copying his dad. But Mitch resisted the urge to smile. He had to remember he had nothing to smile about. Getting saddled with this bit of subterfuge was not his idea of a good time.

Doris was at the checkout counters, putting the cash floats in the tills. He made the introductions, expecting Doris to take over. But she folded her arms and rested her hip against the counter. "Welcome aboard, Maria. We are certainly going to be able to use the extra help." She gave Mitch an insincere, patronizing smile. "You might want to show Maria the staff room, Boss, and let her get rid of her coat." The smile she gave Maria was full of kindness. "You be sure and ask him whatever questions you have when he shows you the layout, hon. And as soon as I'm finished here, we'll decide how we're going to tackle this big shuffle the boss has in mind."

Maria smiled back with that same shyness Mitch had seen earlier; then she turned to him, a look of expectation on her face. He shot Doris an irritated look, then heaved a sigh of resignation and turned toward the staff room. "Come on. I'll show you where you can put your things."

"Mitchell?"

He turned. Maria had a hesitant look on her face as

she whispered so Doris wouldn't hear, "Will you explain 'shuffle'?"

He glanced at his manager, who was acting as if she had important, must-get-it-done business at the tills, then back at Maria. "The way she used it was slang. You understand the meaning of slang?"

Maria nodded, her expression wide-eyed and earnest.

Satisfied with her comprehension, he explained, "Usually it means to mix playing cards. But the way Doris used it means to move things around."

Comprehension dawned. "Ah. To move things around."

Mitch's tone was quiet and reassuring when he counseled her. "Don't be afraid to ask anyone here those kinds of questions, Maria. You'll be working with really good people, and they'll genuinely want to help."

She gave him a little self-conscious shrug, the dimples appearing. "In my country, it is the same. Except sometimes they laugh at mistakes. But reading from books is much easier than speaking the language."

"I'm sure it is." Opening a door, he ushered her inside. "This is the staff room." He explained about the use of the area, and how it was everybody's responsibility to keep it clean, just as he would with any new employee. Or how Doris would normally explain. Damn Doris for dumping this on him. He waited for Maria to carefully hang up her coat. Then he led her through the garden center and out to the greenhouses.

She was keen to learn—that was evident almost immediately. What caught him off guard were the astute questions she asked—questions about the watering system, about how they controlled infestations of various plant pests, the care and management of different stock, the general routine.

What seemed to fascinate her the most was how they heated the enormous glass structures. He explained the forced air systems, with the fans and the large inflatable plastic ducts that moved the warm air. He was careful to use words that would be in her vocabulary, but it still amazed him how quickly she processed information. All this had to be totally new to her, but it was evident she immediately grasped the concepts and mechanics. He remembered the reports from the priest, on what a quick study she was. That certainly hadn't changed.

Doris eventually located them in the second greenhouse, a green smock in her hand identical to the one she was wearing. "Well, I guess we can get started. Karen is here to watch the front end." She handed the smock to Maria. "Here, hon. You put this on. Once we start tearing things apart, we're going to get just filthy. This will save your clothes—at least a little. I wear one all the time." She looked up at Mitchell. "So what's the plan, Stan?"

Maria put on the smock, did up the snaps, then glanced up at Mitch with that same look of expectation he'd noticed earlier. Mitch suddenly felt cornered; he didn't have a plan. He gave Doris a sour look. "You know what you want. Just do it."

Doris cocked one eyebrow and exchanged a long, woman-to-woman look with Maria, one that said all men were daft. Then she gave Mitch a syrupy smile. "Fine. But *you* can knock down those darned metal shelves in the back. I'm not going near those things."

Pointedly ignoring him, she caught Maria around the shoulders. "Come on, hon. We'll strip down the displays and leave him to it. Maybe he can work off his bad temper." She was halfway down the aisle, when she stopped and turned. "And just so you know, the special order of *Sinningia speciosa* finally came in. I had them unload it in the small greenhouse." She started down the aisle again, and Mitch glared at her back. It drove him nuts when she did that. Why couldn't she just have told him in plain English that the shipment of gloxinias had arrived? Why did she always have to turn it into such a big production? Mitch continued to stare after the pair of them, wondering why he kept her on when she gave him nothing but a hard time.

Shaking his head in aggravation, he turned away. Before he started anything inside, he had to finish clearing the parking lot. That was first on his agenda.

By the time he'd cleared the parking lot with the Bobcat and had piled all the snow along the perimeter, he was cold to the bone and ready for a cup of steaming hot coffee.

Not a chance. Like some sort of drill sergeant, Doris pointed him in the direction of the now-empty shelves, then handed him a large screwdriver and a hammer. "Have at 'em, Bossman." Mitch wanted to tell her what she could do with the hammer, screwdriver and all the shelving units, but Maria was standing there, looking like a bright-eyed Miss Innocent.

Feeling suddenly very cranky, Mitch snatched the tools from Doris's hand. He hated dismantling the shelving units as much as she did—maybe even more.

It was always a fight from start to finish, and it was one big, frustrating job. He dragged over one of the big flatbed dollies, then set about knocking the shelves loose, aware that Maria was watching him. He felt like a big, awkward adolescent. He had three shelves off and stacked on the dolly when Karen shouted from the front desk that there was a long distance phone call for him.

It turned out to be one of his suppliers, which meant he had to track down a paper trail in the clutter on his desk and call him back. Dealing with the problem took a good thirty minutes, and Mitch's mood had deteriorated to a new low. And he still had those damned shelves to deal with.

But when he rounded the display of bird feeders and bird seed, he was stopped dead in his tracks. The shelving units had been totally disassembled, and the shelves were all neatly stacked on the big flatbed dolly. Humming to herself, Miss Maria was sweeping up the debris on the floor.

She gave him a beatific smile, then had the audacity to patronize him. "They come apart very easily, Mitchell," she said softly, as if speaking to a dim-witted child, "if you don't whack at them."

He didn't know whether to strangle her or to laugh. He did neither. Instead, he managed a very crisp, businesslike, "Thank you, Maria," trying hard to ignore the big, Cheshire-cat smirk on Doris's face as she stepped into view. He narrowed his eyes, leveling a finger at her in a silent warning. "And not one word out of you, Becker."

Still grinning, she threw up both hands, palms out. "Not a word, Boss. Not one word."

He turned on his heel and walked away. There wasn't a sound, but he knew darned well they were both laughing at him. Just what he needed. Someone else to conspire with Doris behind his back, an ally to play into her warped sense of humor. But there was that same tiny part, the one that had wanted to laugh, that also wanted to feel pretty good. The conspiracy between them meant that Maria had an ally. Not a bad circumstance, considering they had known each other a total of three hours. Not bad at all.

Three whole days passed, and Mitchell managed to avoid the garden center altogether. There was a big home-and-garden show scheduled for the spring, and he had to attend a couple of meetings about that. Then he had to take care of some details concerning a new housing development—one where Murphy had built several homes.

Deliberately trying to avoid detection, Mitch returned to the garden center and went upstairs. After cleaning up his office and clearing off his desk, he spent the better part of a day drafting a very detailed and comprehensive landscape plan.

On Thursday morning, he had a meeting with his banker, but once that was over and done with, he couldn't think of a single, solitary excuse to avoid his place of business any longer. On the way back from the bank, he told himself the reason he'd been avoiding Fairhaven was because he knew it would be one big mess, and in spite of how his office usually looked, that kind of disorder drove him nuts. But a little voice in his head whispered that he was just kidding himself, that that wasn't the reason at all.

When he pulled into the parking lot, there was a large van from one of the seniors' lodges parked at the front door. Mitch closed his eyes and swore. Damn, another detail that had slipped past him. It was Thursday. The day that the seniors came for a visit. And with everything torn apart the way it was, he should have phoned and canceled. The last thing he needed was one of those oldies tripping over something and getting hurt.

He strode in through the glassed-in entrance, then passed through a second sliding door. Once inside, he nearly turned around and walked back out. He didn't recognize the place. Everything had changed. And he had only been gone three days. Not sure his eyes hadn't tricked him, he took a second look.

He couldn't believe it. Everything was in perfect order. There was a quaint little rest area in the dead space beside the downstairs business office. The brand-new setup featured a closed-circulation water fountain and a wrought-iron garden set—a table, chairs and two benches—in a cozy conversational arrangement, all of which was surrounded by bushy palms and flowering hibiscus. It literally screamed warm climes and curb appeal. Charm of the first order. Doris would never have thought of doing something like that if he'd paid her a million bucks and given her ten years to come up with the idea.

His manager was at the front check-out counter serving a customer, and she gave him a big smile and an airy wave, clearly feeling full of herself.

Mitch narrowed his eyes at her. What was going on behind that smug smile? And if she was at the front, who was at the back with the seniors? Because it was usually Doris who volunteered to play hostess to the senior tours.

She read him like a book, giving him another smirk. A nasty feeling of suspicion balled up his gut. Dropping his heavy jacket on one of the park benches, he went through the sliding doors that led to the greenhouses.

The chirp of aged voices was clear above the hum of the heater fans, and he simply followed the sound. And he found out in a glance who the tour guide was. A gardenia blossom tucked behind one ear, her hair a riot of curls around her face and shoulders, a hot-pink blouse hugging her form, Ms. Rogriguez looked like a warm breath of sultry tropic air. And she was clearly charming the hell out of the entire troupe. Mitch stared at her, his breath trapped in his chest.

It was the first time he'd seen her with her hair undone, and it was also the first time he'd seen her in blue jeans. He'd had no idea just how luscious her figure was, or that her hair was so thick and so curly. It was the kind of unruly hair that made a man want to tame it. And that was just her hair. He didn't dare think about the lush curves of her hips and backside molded by the snug-fitting jeans. If he thought about that for more than half a second, he'd end up in really big trouble. Giving his head a shake for that off-the-track and dangerous line of thought, he tried to assimilate the scene before him.

Every single senior was riveted to her every word, but especially engrossed were the four men with the group. Mitch swore he could see them salivating from fifty feet away.

Sheltered behind a grouping of huge palms, he

folded his arms and shook his head, watching her performance, wondering how long it would be before one of the old duffers had a coronary.

Other facts began to click in, and Mitch finally noticed that each member of the group was holding something. Yep. There was no mistake. Each had a four-inch plant pot filled with soil. He considered the pots. They were old containers that had once held various annuals they'd used last season for big arrangements. So, if the pots were nothing but junk, what in hell was she up to?

Maria turned and saw him, a bright smile appearing. ''Ah, Mitchell. Could you help the ladies and gentlemen? Some of them wish to purchase.'' She gave him a disarming little shrug that smacked of pure Latin charm, while somehow managing to look quite helpless. ''But I do not know the care of some of the plants. You will advise them, yes?''

Mitch swept the entire group with a skeptical look. He had set up the seniors' program so old people would have a chance to get out in the middle of winter to enjoy the flowers and tropical setting. And in spite of the hefty discount he offered seniors, he doubted if they had sold more than four plants to any of them in the past five years.

Maria gave him another charming little shrug, then swept her hand toward two double-tray carts parked side by side. There had to be fifteen plants on them—and they weren't tiny little ones. They were all in six-inch pots or bigger.

Feeling as if he was somehow being tested, he stuck a smile on his face and approached the group, his smile becoming genuine when he spotted Gertie at the back of the pack. Gertie was a character, and she had been flirting with him for years.

The withered, gray-haired lady grinned and gave him a sound whack across the shins with her cane. "Well, well. There you are. Now you help this poor young thing out. We've pretty much made a muddle here."

Mitch managed not to wince from the blow. Trying not to laugh, he put his arm around her frail shoulders. "You're putting me on, Gertie. Sounds like you're just working the system."

She chuckled and clipped him again with her cane. "Get away with you." Shuffling her feet and slowly rotating, she pointed to one large plant with her walking stick. "So that's mine. Now what do I do with it?"

Playing the diffident employee, Maria stepped back and folded her hands, an innocent look on her face. Mitch didn't trust that innocence for a minute. But he responded to Gertie's question, giving very explicit directions for care, then did the same with every other plant on the carts. The oldsters clustered around, hanging on every word.

He finished up by asking if there were any questions. No questions. Well, he had a question—but damned if he'd ask it. He was not going to ask about the pots they were all carrying. He figured what he didn't know wouldn't hurt him.

He motioned to Karen, who was watering plants two aisles over, to take one cart, then started toward the checkout area with the other. Maria had given her arm to one of Gertie's lodge mates, and the younger woman was carefully matching her pace to accommodate the old woman, attentive to every word the senior spoke. Mitch experienced an odd clutch in his chest. It was the kind of attentiveness that was based on absolute respect. It reminded him of how solicitous Jordan was with his grandmother, and how considerate. He wasn't sure he was happy with that comparison.

It took them the better part of forty minutes to get everyone and everything bundled up, as well as making sure each wrapped plant was labeled with its new owner's name, and that instructions were included.

But they eventually got the seniors loaded into the van, and Maria remained outside to wave them off. As they pulled away, they all waved back, as if they were a busload of school children off on a brand-new adventure.

Mitch entered the garden center, a shiver running through him. Doris watched him from the cash register, amusement glinting in her eyes. "You aren't going to ask, are you?"

He gave her a blank look. "Ask what?"

"What was in the pots."

He let out a snort and shook his head. "Not in this lifetime."

She grinned. "Well, I'm going to tell you, anyway. Our Maria found some old bulbs when she cleaned out that back corner—as I recall, someone broke a bag last spring and we simply dumped them there in a paper bag. You know the bag I'm talking about?"

For expediency, Mitch nodded.

Doris went on. "Well, Maria also came across that box of old discarded pots, and when she found out about our seniors' days, she had this great idea. Why not use the bulbs and the pots, and give out a planted bulb to each? She thought it would give them something to look forward to, to watch the green shoots come up in the middle of winter. Like spring happening. I gotta tell you, you would have thought she'd given them the moon. Great idea, huh?''

Mitch didn't know why, but Doris's enthusiasm irritated him. ''Great,'' he responded, his tone terse. But he had to set his irritation aside. A member of his staff had taken initiative and done something that deserved recognition. And it had always been his policy to acknowledge that kind of individual effort. It was what good service was all about.

He'd seen Maria come back in and turn toward the greenhouses, and he girded himself and followed her. He found her among the flowering plants, swiftly deadheading wilted blossoms. She still had the gardenia in her hair, and even though she now had on the green smock that covered her hot-pink blouse, there was something very exotic about her. As if something very sultry and mysterious simmered just below the surface. But, hey, lots of other women were equally exotic. He didn't know why, but this woman made him feel as if he was standing on a hot griddle.

He fortified himself with a deep breath. ''Maria.'' She turned, revealing a smear of soil across one cheek. For some reason, he itched to wipe it away. Instead, he stuck his hands in his pockets. ''You did a great job with the seniors today. And giving them the bulbs was a very thoughtful touch.''

There was a hint of anxiety in her eyes. ''It was okay to do?''

He dragged up a small smile. ''Very okay. You

made good use of things we would have eventually thrown out.''

She gave him that now familiar shy smile, accompanied by a self-conscious shrug. ''I thought it would give them something to—'' she looked at him, testing to see if she had the phrase right ''—to look forward to?''

He nodded. ''It will give them something to look forward to. It was an excellent idea.''

She let her breath out in a rush. ''I was not sure.'' Then she grinned. ''But Doris said to go for it.''

Mitch gave her a wry smile. ''Doris would.'' Feeling as if the room was suddenly running out of oxygen, he made an awkward gesture with his hand. ''Well, I'll let you get back to work.''

She gave him the sweetest smile. ''Thank you, Mitchell,'' she said, her voice soft, sensual.

And just like that, in the space of a single heartbeat, he wasn't able to draw a breath at all. Lord, he needed some fresh air. Like a man in a trance, he turned and walked back along the main aisle, parts of his body doing things they had no business doing. He kept telling himself it was nothing. Absolutely nothing. Some electrical impulses had accidentally got short-circuited. That was all. Nothing to worry about. Nothing at all.

But Mitch was not one to dismiss warning signals. He wasn't that big a fool. So over the next few days, he made a point of steering clear of his newest employee if at all possible. He used his head. He thought he had things under control.

But he should have known better. And he should have known something was cooking when his father showed up, all in a froth because Cora had been right, and now they were in one big mess with Immigration. And Mitch should have known he was in big trouble when every one of his siblings made a point to drop in on him at work, trying to draw him into the ongoing melodrama about poor Maria and her plight. Nor did it take someone with a degree in crisis management to figure out the whole damned family was now running around like a proverbial flock of chickens with their heads cut off, flapping their wings, raising a lot of dust. But it was not his problem. Okay, he agreed it was a lousy deal. And it was a damned rotten position to be in, to be so close, then to have all your dreams totally shattered. But there was not one darn thing he could do about it. It was out of his hands.

It was, he discovered, not an opinion shared by all.

He found that out when he was coerced into attending a family meeting at Murphy's. Mitch was sitting there, filling his required space, minding his own business and listening to them try to come up with a miracle solution for the Rodriguezes. There had been a huge debate on when they were going to tell Maria where she stood—some thinking they couldn't keep her in the dark much longer, others insisting that they say nothing until they were darned sure they had exhausted all their options.

Cora, her face flushed and her eyes flashing with a mix of frustration and annoyance, simply raised her voice and talked over the top of everybody else. "Look, you guys," she said, determined to make herself heard. "You aren't listening to me. I'm telling you, there is nothing we can do about it. We're going to have to tell Maria the truth. They aren't going to be able to stay, no matter what scheme we come up with. You just can't break the rules. And the rules say she can't apply for landed immigrant status from within the country. You're going to have to face the facts that sooner or later she has to be told.''

His grandmother, his big-hearted, kind but equally sly, scheming and devious Baba, waved off Cora's assertions, then looked at him with a cunning smile. ''There is answer to problem. Mitch should marry her.''

Mitchell stared at her as if she had just launched herself out of a cannon, shock waves of horror shooting right down to his toes. One thing was for sure— Baba knew how to get everyone's attention.

As if someone had pulled the plug on all the chatter, the rest of the family went dead silent. Except Murphy. Murphy had the damned nerve to laugh. ''Hey. That sounds like one hell of a plan, Baba. We'll kill two birds with one stone. We'll rescue Maria and marry off old Mitch.''

Mitch cast his brother a scathing look, and Baba held up her hand for silence, nodding her head. Baba was a war bride, Ukrainian by birth, and she had no qualms about being outrageous. She saw that Mitch was about to tell his brother where he could go and how fast, and she turned her palm in his direction. ''Is good plan. Mitchell needs wife. Maria needs husband. Would work.''

Mitch stared at her, a strangling sensation making the blood pound in his head. Without saying a single word, he got to his feet, picked up his coat and stomped out of the room, wondering what in hell had gotten into that little old lady. Hell, she was treating this whole thing as if it were some sort of crazy game.

Stamping his feet into his boots, he swore under his breath. And from Murphy's living room, he could hear Baba's voice, deliberately loud so he could hear, and clear as a bell. ''Is a good plan. I know.''

Feeling as if he were drowning and about to go down for the third and final time, he slammed out of the house, rattling all the windows in the process. God, no wonder he hated these family get-togethers. They were all a bunch of loonies.

He expected better. He thought his family, among the lot of them, should be able to produce at least one single shred of common sense. But oh, no. By the end of the week, all his sisters had climbed on the Baba Bandwagon. And Mitch began to wish he were an orphan. Okay. He had to be honest with himself here. It wasn't as if Maria made his stomach curdle or anything—in fact, she was a damned attractive woman, with those huge brown eyes and that fantastic head of black, shiny hair. And he had to admit that that Latin voluptuousness of hers had him thinking things he had no business thinking.

Hell, he even liked her two stepsons. And it wasn't as if he was such a hard-hearted bastard that he had no empathy for her situation. He had all kinds of empathy.

In fact, he figured her situation was pretty bloody awful. But would he even entertain the idea of marrying her as part of a rescue mission? Not in this lifetime. He'd tried that once, and it had been a disaster, and that time he'd been head-over-heels in love with the woman. He'd learned the hard way that some men just weren't cut out for marriage. And he was one of them.

Hell, he didn't even *know* this woman. And since she'd arrived, he'd made a point of keeping it that way. Okay, she'd been on the periphery of the family for a long time, but really, she'd consisted of nothing more than long-distance reports and a series of pictures that had progressed, year by year, across the top of the family piano. And yeah, he noticed her around the greenhouse, even though he tried not to. But marry her? Not a chance.

What in hell did they expect from him? He'd given her a job, and in the process, broken enough immigration and labor laws to get himself tossed in jail for a very long time. But he'd been prepared to stick his neck out. He'd been raised with values. And he sincerely believed it was a moral responsibility for everyone to lend a helping hand to those less fortunate. But that philosophy didn't extend to marriage. Not while he still had breath in him.

When it finally became obvious that Mitch wasn't going to be part of the solution, the entire Munroe family tried to come up with various other insane ideas that would allow the Rodriguezes to stay past their time limitation. Mitch dealt with the ever-expanding fracas by systematically removing himself from the line of fire. There were just too many figurative bullets whining around his head.

In fact, he hardly thought about it at all. He had better things to worry about.

Like the shipment of small tropical plants that had suffered considerable damage in transit. It wasn't really that big of a deal. The shipment was covered by insurance, and rather than pay the cost of shipping them back, the supplier had simply written off the entire load, and left it up to Mitch to dispose of the mess. They had them all off-loaded into the smaller greenhouse to free up the semi, and he had intended on sending the load out to the dump. But his newest employee had other ideas.

It was midafternoon when Mitch discovered her in the small greenhouse, sorting through the plants. But she wasn't alone. She had Grandfather Rodriguez with her. There was a long potting bench at the back covered with bits and pieces of old floral adornments, lumps of moss, chunks of bark, pieces of broken pottery.

Sitting on the floor next to the potting table was a large tub of steaming water, and Grandfather had a bunch of battered old willow baskets soaking in it. As Mitchell watched, the old man lifted out one of the baskets that had been presoaked, and with quick-as-lightning speed and adept hands, he reshaped the basket, then pressed it into a form he had constructed out of some old wood. It became obvious that the two of them were running a salvage operation with the bits and pieces of flotsam and fauna that everyone else had tossed out. Shaking his head, Mitch gave a tired sigh. It was a waste of time. But if it made them happy, what the hell.

He was about to turn and walk away, leaving them to it, when Maria moved, and Mitch got a look at the end product. He could not believe his eyes.

They might be working with nothing but rubbish, but Maria had somehow managed to take all those bits and pieces—the damaged plants and the battered baskets—and turn them into the most amazing arrangements he had ever seen. This miracle worker was turning pigs' ears into silk purses. She was spinning straw into pure gold. Yeah, the plants were looking kind of scrawny, but in a few weeks, when they started to fill out, the baskets would be spectacular.

Forgetting about his resolution to stay clear of her, he entered the work area. The old man looked up and grinned, his eyes twinkling, his face creasing into a network of lines and wrinkles. Mitch got a kick out of the old man, and he smiled back and raised his hand in salutation. Maria, on the other hand, was oblivious.

"You've been very busy, Maria."

She jumped and turned, her hand clamped against her chest, but instead of alarm, he saw what appeared to be guilt in her eyes. As if she'd been caught doing something she shouldn't. She licked her lips and managed a weak smile. "Mitchell."

Now why in hell did she have to go and lick her lips? They were full and ripe, just like the rest of her, and Mitch's attention was riveted on her mouth. He could feel his blood start to thicken and heat. Annoyed at himself and his lousy attention span, he forced his gaze higher. The guilt was still there, and that bothered him, making him almost angry. And that reaction didn't make any sense at all. Rather than let her see his response, he closed off his expression and said nothing.

His silence clearly unsettled her even more, and she made a nervous gesture toward the arrangement. "I thought I would make a…sample. Yes, I think that is the right word—that I would make some samples to show you. So you could save the damaged plants. It will take two, maybe three weeks and they will be very nice again.''

Her sudden uncertainty about how he was going to react made his insides shrivel, and he anchored his hands in his pockets to keep from touching her. With some unexpected insight, he realized she didn't understand about the shipper carrying insurance, and she was trying to help Mitch recoup his losses. The realization made his chest tighten and a funny sensation start unfolding deep in his belly. It had been a long time since anyone had looked out for his interests or had any concerns on his behalf. A very long time. That realization rocked him like little else ever had.

It was all he could do to hold her gaze, and his voice was gruff when he spoke. ''They are very nice. And I'm sure they'll sell well.''

Her eyes brightened. ''Yes? You think so?''

Feeling as if he had a large obstruction wedged in his throat, he nodded. ''Definitely. You're doing an excellent job.''

She turned to the old man and spoke to him in rapid Spanish, and the grandfather smiled, his face crinkling. ''Is good,'' he said.

Mitch managed a small smile in return, then started to walk away. But a brainstorm hit, an idea about improving her finances. He thought about it for an instant, then turned back to Maria. ''Tell you what,'' he said, giving her a steady look. ''I'm going to make you a business deal.''

She gave him a wary look. ''A business deal?''

He indicated the baskets. ''You showed a lot of initiative…'' He paused, frowning at her. ''Do you understand *initiative?*''

She gave him an offended look. "It is in my meager vocabulary, yes."

The corner of his mouth wanted to lift for some reason, but he didn't acknowledge her fit of pique. He simply continued. "So. Since you came up with the plan to make use of this stuff, this is the deal. We'll split the profits fifty-fifty."

She cocked her hip and folded her arms, then tipped her head to one side and glared at him. "No, Mitchell. I do not think so. No fifty-fifty. You already pay my wage."

For some oddball reason, he wanted to laugh. Then, just as suddenly, he was annoyed by her response and equally annoyed at her for defying him. Not hiding his irritation, he jammed his hands on his hips and glared right back at her. "Look. It would have all gone in the garbage if it hadn't been for your *initiative*. It's the way I do business, Maria. And it's called profit sharing." He narrowed his eyes, challenging her. "So you can either take it or—"

The old man, who'd been following the exchange, his attention bobbing from one to the other like a spry little bird, interjected. "We take it." Laying a restraining hand on Maria's arm, he nodded and grinned at Mitchell. "We do…business the Canada way."

Maria turned to him and said something in rapid Spanish, obviously trying to persuade her father-in-law to her way of thinking. Grandfather waved his finger at her in a gesture of gentle chastisement and said something back to her, his tone soft but scolding. There was another exchange, and it was pretty obvious the old man was advising her on the ways of the world. Maria stared at her father-in-law for a moment,

then capitulated with a resigned sigh. She turned back
to Mitch and lifted her chin, clearly drawing upon her
pride. "Grandfather insists. We will do business your
way."

Holding her gaze, Mitch studied her, a twist of
amusement surfacing. "Fine," he said, watching her
face. "I'll give Doris the details." As he turned and
walked away, he heard her mutter something in Spanish that definitely sounded disgruntled. He grinned. If
this arrangement continued, he was going to have to
level out the playing field and learn Spanish.

Of course, the entire business plan backfired in his
face. The next morning, not only did Grandfather
show up for work, but so did the two boys, and it was
pretty clear that the "business deal" had been dis-
cussed and had turned into a family affair. Mitch felt
as if he had been caught from behind by an avalanche
and was suddenly buried up to his neck. Just what he
needed. More illegals working for him. He didn't dare
think about what Immigration would do to him if they
showed up and found not one, but four Latin Americans up to their armpits in potting soil.

He shuddered just thinking about it. But he wearily
shook his head and resigned himself, deciding he
might as well be hung for a sheep as a lamb. When
he talked to Maria about hiring the boys as part-time
help, however, she wouldn't even hear him out. A deal
was a deal.

His only recourse was to try to turn a blind eye to
what was going on, and to avoid the situation if at all
possible. But that was easier said than done. Especially
when he found the boys actually *dusting* the slat shelving where the baskets were arranged. And there wasn't

a withered blossom or a dead leaf anywhere. The entire place had never been so clean and tidy, swept and dusted. He knew Maria was passing out orders to the boys behind his back, but he couldn't catch them at it. It was as if he had acquired two new invisible plant elves. Of course, it didn't help matters that Doris and the rest of his staff kept gushing about how wonderful the Rodriguezes were. In fact, he found it damned annoying.

As much as he tried to turn a blind eye, there were some things he couldn't ignore. Maria's English, which she had used off and on in her years of service to wealthy Americans, was improving by leaps and bounds. Doris started putting up a daily vocabulary list in the staff room, and the entire crew got into the game, going to ridiculous lengths to use the posted words. Mitch figured there were at least two of his employees who were expanding their own vocabularies right along with Maria, so he considered the nonsense some sort of weird employee benefit. It got so out of control that even some of the regular customers became involved in the craziness.

But that was only part of it. Although Maria spent a portion of her time in the potting sheds supervising the "business deal," she had practically taken over running the greenhouses, not to mention the garden center. They got so much accomplished with her on staff, he wasn't sure how they'd ever managed without her.

And as much as he might have wanted to, he could not ignore Maria's genuine aptitude with the customers. She had this capacity to—hell, he couldn't even define it for himself—but she had this capacity to *en-*

gage with nearly every single customer she served. She treated the seniors with the utmost respect and consideration, and they loved her. The female customers gravitated to her because of her humor and uncanny ability to know what they wanted, as well as her ability to conspire with them. And the men—well, Mitch didn't even want to think about the men. He couldn't count how many he'd come across fixed and speechless, like great dumb garden statues, their eyes and tongues hanging out, riveted to the ground by her obvious womanly attributes. And he didn't know why, but for some reason, he wanted to smack every single one of them with his long-handled spade.

But did he make it his business to find out what else was going on? Not a chance. As far as the Rodriguezes were concerned, he was deaf, dumb and blind. And he was quite happy that way. He liked not knowing anything. He didn't want to get involved. Besides, it fit with his image of being a bad-tempered recluse.

Yep, he was doing just fine. He was impervious. No ties. No connections.

But that all came crashing to an end when he witnessed a quiet family tableau very early one morning, in one dusky corner of the potting shed.

He was about to give Maria hell for them all being at work so early, but there was something about their intentness, about how they were standing clustered together in a single unit, that stopped him. It was as if they were all united in a common cause. Then he saw what was going on, and a strange, ballooning feeling unfolded in his chest. And he stood there, unable to move, unable to turn away.

It was one of the scenes that stuck in a person's

mind, one of those mental images that would never go away, and Mitch knew it was one that was going to stay with him for a very, very long time.

Grandfather was seated on a stack of wooden flats, with one shoe off. And Roberto, the sixteen-year-old, was trying to cut an insole from a discarded piece of rubber matting. Maria and Enrico were watching him, and Maria was at his shoulder, giving him quiet instructions in Spanish. Even with the density of shadows, even from the distance of the doorway, Mitch could see the crack in the sole of the old man's shoe. A common cause, all right. Like grinding poverty. Like making do.

The ballooning sensation got worse, clogging up his chest and making his throat cramp. What would it be like, he thought, to have so little, and to know that your chances of a better life hinged on a lifelong dream? A dream that had about a million-to-one chance of surviving? Three people clustered like planets around this one woman, three people who depended on her to make their life better.

Feeling lower than a snake, Mitch turned, experiencing a rush of self-loathing. Lord, but he deserved a damned good shaking. He'd been so stuck on maintaining his status quo that he hadn't even seen the whole big picture. Yeah. He'd been some hero, all right.

What he'd really been was one cold, hard-hearted, unfeeling bastard.

Chapter 4

It was pure bedlam. For Mitch, it was like being trapped in a stadium crowd at some major sports event. Only this didn't have anything to do with sport. This had to do with survival. This was a Sunday dinner at the Munroe house.

At last one of the women—probably his mother—fired the starter gun and called out that dinner was ready. Like the passing of a torch, the announcement was immediately relayed from person to person, room to room, and finally down the stairs to the family room below. And like the start of some marathon race, family members started converging and scrambling up the stairs, the din of voices in the kitchen rising over the clatter of dishes and the shrieks of children. Mitch tried to shrink into the corner beside the big double fridge, a can of beer clutched in his hand, the crush of claustrophobia pushing in on him.

With the windows fogged with condensation from the steaming pots on the stove, the kitchen blazed with lights, the brightness and sudden traffic jam effectively pinning him to the wall. The raucous chatter raked across his nerves, and he could feel a prickle of sweat in his hair and down his back. It took all he could do to anchor his feet on the floor to keep from bolting. God, but he hated these Sunday get-togethers. All he could say was that he was glad they weren't a weekly event.

Even so, he would have found some excuse to stay away this time, but his sister Jessica had phoned up and specifically asked him to come. Jessica hardly ever asked anything of him, so out of his sense of duty to her, he had come. And now he was wishing he hadn't.

It wasn't as if he didn't care about his family. He did—and would have gladly laid down his life for any single one of them. It was just that there were so many. And the group kept getting bigger all the time. There were his parents and Baba, then Murphy, Jordan and their two kids, with another one on the way. Jessica and Marco and their three kids, with a fourth one also due. Finally there were the twins and their spouses. Cora and Martin didn't have any kids, but Caroline and Jake now had three. Throw the four Rodriguezes into the pot, and the whole mess gave him a serious case of claustrophobia. He felt as if he was about to suffocate. He could manage one on one—he could handle that with no problem at all. He could even handle them in small groups. But the whole lot of them together, in one room in the middle of winter, when he couldn't even escape outside—it was enough to make him break out in a cold sweat.

It wasn't really the numbers. It was the Munroe pack mentality. Mitch would be willing to bet his next year's total gross that at some point during the evening, when they had run out of other targets, someone would line their sights up on him and fire off some opinionated comment about him and his life-style. Then they would all pile on, like a bunch of unruly kids playing tackle football. No wonder his brother Cameron worked in South America—it was one sure way to get out of attending these family cattle calls. But Jessica had specifically phoned and asked him to please come. And even he wasn't a big enough louse to opt out on her. Not when she had that tone in her voice.

Forcing himself to stay calm, he downed the rest of the beer, wishing it was straight Scotch. Maybe that would fortify him enough to get through the next couple of hours.

Feeling a hand on his arm, he looked down to see Jordan beside him, his nephew Eric on her hip. She was watching Mitch with a twinkle in her eyes and amusement lurking around her mouth. Somehow or another, she'd picked up on how he felt about these family mob scenes, and she acted as if she actually understood. The twinkle intensifying, she gave his arm a comforting pat. "Hang in there, big guy. I think you're safe tonight."

He gave her a small wry smile. "Would you put that in writing?"

Her son grinned and jabbered something, then reached for Mitch with one hand. She wiped the little one's nose with a tissue, then handed him over to his uncle. She met Mitch's gaze, her eyes dancing. "I'm not offering you a contract, Mitchell. I'm just giving you my opinion.'' She straightened the straps on her son's overalls, then tickled his belly, eliciting a hearty chuckle. Smiling, she chucked Eric under the chin; then she glanced up at Mitch, her gaze turning serious. ''The reason you're safe is that I think everyone has other things on their mind.''

''What other things?''

She gave a little shrug. ''I guess Cora had it out with your mom and dad this afternoon, about them keeping Maria in the dark. She insisted that they had to tell her what was going on.''

''Did they?''

Jordan sighed and nodded. ''Well, sort of. I guess they forewarned her that there could be a problem.''

Mitch experienced a funny sensation in his chest, and his own gaze sobered. ''How did she take it?''

Jordan gave another halfhearted shrug and fussed with the bib on Eric's overalls. ''Stoically. But maybe not as realistically as she should. From what your mom said, I don't think Maria's going to say anything to the boys.'' Jordan looked up at Mitch, her eyes dark with concern. ''I expect she's hoping for some kind of miracle.'' She managed a weak smile and reached up to smooth her son's hair. ''I can't say I blame her.''

Someone called Jordan's name and she turned, then glanced back at Mitch, indicating her son. ''Can I leave him with you?''

Mitch nodded, and a hint of humor lightened Jordan's eyes as she warned him, ''Don't you dare let him out of your sight. He's decided he has a mission, and none of Grandma's plants are safe. I think he's spent too much time at the greenhouse, watching his uncle Mitch. He thinks he has to transplant everything.''

Mitch chuckled. "If he's still interested, maybe I can give him a job in the spring."

Jordan rolled her eyes, giving her son a tap on the end of his nose. "You be good for Uncle Mitch."

Mitch watched her cross to the work island and take a large plastic container from Jessica; then he glanced down at his nephew. Eric was intently trying to poke his chubby finger in the opening of Mitch's empty beer. Just what he needed—the kid getting his finger stuck in a beer can. Wise to the ways of children, Mitch set the can on the telephone table.

Eric gave him a scowl, then tried to poke his finger in his uncle's ear. Mitch caught the kid's hand and tried to distract him with a one-handed game of patty-cake, but Eric wasn't having any of that silly baby stuff. Giving his uncle a mischievous grin, he pulled his hand free and immediately tried to poke his finger up Mitch's nose. Growling and making a face, Mitch upended him, and Eric squealed with delight, reaching his arms down toward the floor.

Mitch lowered him until he was able to touch, then swung him back up. Eric squealed again. It was an old game, and the kid loved it. Mitch humored him and did it a couple more times, then he flipped the kid up on his shoulders, his chubby legs straddling Mitch's head. He grinned to himself. Jordan didn't need to warn him. He knew from experience that the only way to make sure this kid didn't get into any trouble was to keep him six feet off the ground.

His grin froze when he saw Maria watching him from across the kitchen, the oddest smile on her face.

Mitch experienced a strange off-the-ground feeling, and he looked away. Hell, he must be more out of shape than he thought—ten minutes of horsing around with his nephew, and his lungs were caving in on him.

Dinner was like feeding time at the zoo. There were simply too many of them for a civilized dinner, so it was all served buffet. Grandma Munroe had a rule about kids walking around with food, so the little ones all sat at the huge kitchen table, along with Baba and a sprinkling of adults. The rest filled their plates and sat wherever. Mitchell followed suit, then found a quiet corner in the living room. Roberto and Enrico followed him in, both of them looking a little bit dazed. Mitch figured they were probably feeling just as overwhelmed by the masses of Munroes as he was. He gave them a lopsided smile. "You guys can hide out in here if you like. It's a little too nuts out there for me."

Enrico, the fourteen-year-old, hardly ever said anything in his presence, but he was Mitch's shadow at the greenhouses. He gave Mitchell a shy, lopsided smile and sat next to him on the floor, his back braced against the sofa.

Far more outgoing, and possessing more charm than any kid that age had a right to have, Roberto gave him a big grin and sat on the floor in front of the fireplace. "There are many people here. The kitchen is like a soccer field, yes?"

Mitch grinned and nodded his head. "You got that right." He figured that was a pretty apt description.

Noticing the clothes the boys had on, Mitch experienced a funny hollow feeling in his gut. The kids had practically nothing—one good set of clothes each, definitely not new, and a couple of well-worn outfits they wore to work.

He would have liked to have done something for them sooner, but he was afraid that Maria would see it as charity. But both boys had birthdays coming up, and that would be his excuse to take them shopping. And since Maria had put her foot down about the boys accepting wages, Mitch could turn the tables on her and insist that the clothes were his way of reimbursing them. He knew darned well she wouldn't like it, but that was just too bad. Besides, he didn't have anything to spend his money on, and it wouldn't kill him to cough up a few bucks. And damn it, they deserved some decent things.

They ate in silence, with the boys quietly exchanging a few comments in Spanish, and Mitch pretending not to notice. He wasn't avoiding conversation; what he was trying to do was figure out how to get a specific conversation started without coming across as just plain nosy. And maybe he was being nosy, but he was damned curious.

When the boys had started showing up at the garden center, Doris had come up with as many odd jobs as she could possibly find for them. And Maria made sure they also found things to do, prompting Roberto about offering to carry a heavy plant out to the car for an older woman, for example.

The woman had tipped Roberto, and the teenager had promptly brought the tip to Mitch. Enrico had been there as well, and Mitch had told the boys that the tips were theirs to keep. The two teenagers had been unusually animated about this. As Mitch watched, Enrico and Roberto had gone to Maria, and after some lengthy explanation, Roberto had given the gratuity to his stepmother. What had Mitch curious was that it hadn't been just a straightforward case of giving money to Mom—it was as if some kind of plan had been hatched.

Mitch's attention refocused when the boys switched to English, and they started talking about a soccer game they had seen on TV. Enrico made a comment that he hoped they'd have a soccer team at the school they'd be attending.

Mitch stopped eating, his expression turning thoughtful as he watched them now. It was pretty obvious they were unaware that they would likely never attend school here. His appetite suddenly gone, Mitch set his plate on the coffee table and slouched down, lacing his hands across his chest.

Trying to ignore the disquieting feeling, he changed the subject. His tone was deliberately offhand when he spoke. "How would you guys like to learn how to drive?"

Their heads jerked around in unison, eyes wide with anticipation. Roberto grinned. "We would like that very much."

A hint of a smile surfaced as Mitch studied them. "You have to get a learner's license here before you can drive. And you have to pass an exam before you get the permit."

Roberto and his brother exchanged a look, then Enrico spoke up. "An exam?"

Mitch nodded. "An examination. A test. But it's not really a big deal. The government provides manuals for you to study, and if you know everything that's in the book, you'll pass the exam."

Roberto's eyes were glinting with excitement. "How do we get this manual, Mitchell?"

Mitch gave them a wry grin. "Well, if you check the inside pocket of my coat, you just might find a couple."

They set down their plates and scrambled, jostling each other to get to the closet first. Mitch watched, amused by their enthusiasm. Boys and cars—some things never changed.

Maria spotted them digging through Mitch's coat, and she came into the hallway, severely scolding them in Spanish. Mitch interceded on the kids' behalf. "It's okay, Maria. I picked up some stuff for them, and it's in my pocket. I told them they could get it."

She glanced at him, then back at Enrico when he rattled off an explanation in Spanish, his face flushed with excitement. Maria looked at Mitchell, clearly uncertain about all this. He tried to reassure her. "Don't get in a panic, Mother. They have to pass an exam first."

Wiping her hands down her thighs, she tried to smile. Mitch recognized the anxiety in her body language and the worry lines around her eyes, and he experienced an unsettling reaction. She had so much on her shoulders, and now the dream of being able to stay in Canada was in serious jeopardy. It must have been one hell of a blow. He wondered just how panicky she was feeling inside.

Ignoring his internal caution signals, he indicated the other end of the sofa. "Hey, sit down, and don't worry about it. They have a long way to go before they get turned loose with a vehicle, Maria."

Maria gave him another weak smile and made a

nervous gesture with her hands, and a lightbulb suddenly went on in Mitch's head. There was more to this than just the driving; on top of everything else, she was probably worrying about what this was going to cost.

Wanting to skirt that issue if at all possible, he out-and-out lied. "And it isn't going to cost them anything to write the exam. They won't likely pass the first time, anyway." Which he'd bet a month's sales would not be the case. He'd seen enough of the boys to know darned well they were going to know that manual inside and out, and there wasn't a chance in hell they would fail. But she didn't need to know that. "It's not a big deal."

She kicked off her shoes and sat on the other end of the sofa, then drew up her knees and wrapped her arms around her legs. She gave him a pointed look. "It is a very big deal, Mitchell," she said, indicating the boys, who were huddled together in front of the fireplace, going through the manuals. "At least for them."

Resting his head against the back of the sofa, Mitchell propped his feet on the coffee table and crossed his ankles. He gave her what he hoped was a reassuring smile. "Well, just so you don't get yourself in a panic, I've got a tree farm a couple of hours north of here, and as soon as it dries up a bit, I'm going to take 'em out there and turn 'em loose. They can practice driving in the fields until they get the hang of it. With that kind of space, they won't be able to do much damage to anything, including themselves."

A twinkle appeared in her eyes. "So you believe, Mitchell. This you do not know for certain."

"I'm pretty sure."

Her smile faded and there was a distracted look in her eyes, her expression turning anxious. She looked as if she hadn't had much sleep.

But what bothered him most was that she looked so damned worried, so alone. He'd had a whole lot of experience with aloneness and had a pretty good idea what she must be feeling right now. And being told she was probably going to have to go back to their old life didn't help. It made him feel pretty lousy. Normally he would have gotten up and walked away, but he could not bring himself to abandon her right then. Without thinking about what he was doing, Mitch reached over and gave her wrist a squeeze. "Everything is going to be okay," he said quietly, trying to bolster her, even though he knew it was not okay. "Try not to worry, all right?"

Her eyes filled with tears and she started to get up, but Mitch tightened his hold, and suddenly—he didn't even know how it happened—he was holding her hand. Her fingers tightened around his in a desperate grip as she stared at him, her eyes brimming with despair.

Then she abruptly dropped his hand, got up and practically ran out of the room. Nailed with a heavy-duty sense of guilt, Mitch tipped his head back and closed his eyes, a terrible thickness unfolding in his chest. He should have never touched her. That was one rule he had no business breaking. His hand still tingled from the heat of her, and he wiped it against his thigh. Obviously, there were a whole lot of rules he'd better not break.

* * *

The following morning was not so hot. A Chinook had blown in in the middle of the night and there was a smell of spring in the air, no matter how false the promise was. The renovations were all done and everything was shipshape. Even Mitch knew that the first hint of spring always brought the customers out.

But the truth was, he felt like hell. He got up with the dull, headachy feeling of being hungover, which was okay, if he had been hungover. But he wasn't. Of course, the fact that his sleep had been repeatedly interrupted by dreams didn't help. Disturbing dreams he couldn't quite remember that left him with bits and pieces of images. Maria reaching out to him as darkness swallowed her. Maria grasping his hand. Maria calling to him from the darkness. Dumb stuff. Stuff that didn't make sense. Stuff that left him feeling empty and alone.

Lucky for Mitch, the outdoor compound where they stockpiled bulk inventory during the summer—various kinds of fertilizer, decorative crushed rock and big bags of grass seed—needed to be cleaned up and rearranged. And with a Chinook settled in for the next few days, it was a perfect time to do it. It wasn't as if he was using it as an excuse to avoid the garden center.

He was roaring around on the Bobcat with the forklift on it, stacking the last of the old shipping pallets, when Doris came out the side door, her smock pulled around her. She yelled at him to quit messing around with his motorized toys, that they needed him inside.

Experiencing a definite reluctance about having to go in, Mitch finished stacking the pallets, then parked the Bobcat in one of the storage sheds.

From where he was working behind the green-houses, he'd heard the traffic sounds and knew there had been a lot of coming and going in the parking lot. And even though years of experience proved that a spring Chinook brought hopeful gardeners out in droves, he wasn't expecting it to be quite so busy. He also knew that there was no point in calling extra staff; by the time someone got there, the rush would likely be over. So he manned one of the checkouts, ringing through packets of seeds, potted arrangements of spring bulbs and stacks of gardening books.

He had just closed down his register and was head-ing upstairs to his office when Roberto reentered the garden center. The teenager had just finished loading a dozen large plants in a minivan for Millie Black, an interior designer who had purchased plants for four model homes she was decorating. Mitch smiled to himself when he saw the distinctive blue of a five-dollar bill in the kid's hand. Millie had been buying plants from Fairhaven Nurseries for at least ten years, and Mitch was willing to bet she had never tipped any of the help before.

Roberto caught him watching, and he gave Mitch a very macho shrug and a sheepish grin. "I called her Miss—I think she liked it."

Millie had to be at least fifty years old, and that was cutting her a whole lot of slack. Mitch chuckled and slapped the boy on the back. "That will do it every time." Ignoring a twinge of guilty conscience for be-ing a snoop, he used the opportunity to do exactly that. "So what are you and Enrico doing with your tip money, blowing it on girls?"

Roberto laughed and held up his hands in a gesture

of denial, his black eyes flashing. "No. No. We do not know any girls, Mitchell."

Mitch knew he should be totally disgusted with himself, but he pushed, anyway. "Then what?"

The boy's expression sobered and he looked away. "We give it to our *madre*—to our mother. We are saving to get a place of our own to live." He gave another discomfited shrug, then bent down and picked a scrap of paper off the floor.

He still didn't look at Mitch as he wadded it up into a tight little ball. "My mother has a big responsibility, and we want to help. She says we have taken..." He paused, searching for the correct words before continuing, "she says we have taken advantage of the hospitality of your family for too long. So we are saving for that." He looked at Mitch and flashed him a wide smile, indicating the sliding doors that led to the greenhouse. "Now I must go move plants." He grinned again, a glint of mischief in his black eyes. "Doris has given me many instructions."

Mitch nodded and forced a smile in response, but his expression turned sober as he watched the boy walk away, a knot the size of a grapefruit forming in his belly. Needing time alone to process what the kid had told him, Mitch opted for the stairs, the feeling in his gut expanding.

He entered his office and quietly shut and locked the door behind him; then he went over to stand before the window, finally allowing himself a reaction. Two kids. Saving the pittance they made on tips so they could get a place of their own. To help their mother. He recalled the scene in the potting shed, the four of them huddled together, cutting out an insole for

Grandfather's shoe. Mitch's chest got tight and his throat hurt. Life shouldn't be that hard. And there wasn't a damned thing he could do about it, at least not without offending Maria. She didn't want charity. All she wanted was a decent chance for her boys. A chance she wasn't likely to get.

But there was more to it than that. It was hard to believe that she was their stepmother—that they weren't hers by birth. Clearly she was their mother in every sense of the word, and it was obvious that the boys and her father-in-law were devoted to her. But what really got to Mitch was the fact that she wasn't all that much older than Roberto—fourteen years at most. Yet a lifetime of responsibility separated them.

His throat got even tighter and he gouged his eyes with his thumb, then straightened. Maybe those basket arrangements would fetch another few bucks each. He wished to hell he'd tried to split the profits more in her favor. But he'd been pretty darned certain at the time that the fifty-fifty split was the maximum she'd accept. And that hadn't changed. But there wasn't anything stopping him from raising the price. He could up the profit. Maybe he could push them up another ten.

Then there was the empty apartment across the hall from his—the one he had developed years ago for an on-site manager. But the original manager had left and Doris had come on board. The apartment had been used only sporadically since, mostly as overflow accommodation for family members and some of Doris's relatives. Right now, it was empty. But he'd bet his life that Maria would never go for that. Not in a million years.

* * *

The whole thing with Maria had gotten too close, too personal somehow. And Mitch knew he had to disconnect. So he made a snap decision to spend a few days at the tree farm. Deciding he needed an accurate accounting of his inventory, he and his manager compiled an account that was so detailed, it practically itemized weeds. When they finished with that, Mitch started selecting specific stock for the spring season. His manager thought he was nuts. Mitch was beginning to think so, too.

Normally he viewed the time he spent there as a bit of a break from his regular routine, but this time, it was more of an escape. And he wasn't even sure what he was escaping from. Himself, most likely. Having the Rodriguezes around had knocked off some old scabs, and he didn't like the feeling. It made him feel exposed.

And he kept thinking about their hoarding money in a can to come to Canada. About them saving every red cent so they could get a place of their own. It was about dignity, about pride, about making it on their own. Mitch spent more sleepless nights than he could count, thinking about them wanting nothing more than a chance. His reflections weren't comfortable ones, especially when he had squandered so many chances in his own life. It didn't make him feel very good about a whole lot of things.

It was the last week of March when he finally returned to Calgary. And he wasn't too sure he even wanted to go back then, but he couldn't, in good conscience, stretch it out any longer. He'd dumped everything on Doris's shoulders for too long as it was.

By the time he rolled into the parking lot, it was

well after ten o'clock, but even in the dark, he could
see how the piles of snow had shrunk. If he was reading the signs right, it was going to be an early spring.
But right then, he was so damned tired, he didn't really
care.

Taking off hadn't solved anything. Especially when
he had made it his mission to check every damned
tree and shrub on the place. Consequently, he had
walked mile after mile, most of it on snowshoes. By
the time he crawled out of the Jeep, he felt as if someone had beaten his legs with a stick. All he wanted
was a decent bed and about ten hours of sleep.

He got seven. Murphy and Cora were at his door
before the sun was barely up. He dragged on a pair of
jeans to answer the loud knocking and gave them a
baleful look. Leaving the apartment door only partly
ajar with the hopes that they might not come in, he
turned toward the kitchen. "God," he snapped.
"Hasn't this family got anything better to do with its
time?"

He heard the door close as he started running water
for coffee. Cora's perfume preceded her into the
kitchen. He heard a chair scrape, but he continued to
pretend they weren't there. If this were a normal family, they wouldn't be. He finished making coffee, then
stuck his head under the cold tap to try and wake up,
the shock of the icy water brutally clearing away the
cobwebs. His internal radar told him he was going to
have to be wide-awake and on his guard for whatever
these two were trotting in.

He snatched up a hand towel and roughly towel-
dried his hair, then draped it around his neck. Not even
trying to hide his annoyance, he turned and leaned

back against the counter, folding his arms. He didn't say anything, just stared at them. Cora had the decency to squirm. But not Murphy. His brother was leaning against the far wall in the exact same stance as Mitchell. Murphy gave him a big grin. "Happy, happy Mitchy."

Mitch fixed him with an uncharitable look. "Drop dead."

Cora was twisting the strap of her handbag, a worried look in her eyes. "Mitch. We might have a problem."

"No, *we* don't," he snapped, putting heavy emphasis on the "we."

She acted like she didn't hear him. "I finally persuaded Dad that they were going to have to see an immigration lawyer, only he got into an argument with him yesterday, and I'm afraid Dad isn't going to listen. If Dad goes off half-cocked, he could stir up more trouble than we know what to do with."

Mitch looked from her to Murphy, then back to Cora. Then he made his point. "I already have more trouble than I know what to do with. And it isn't even 8:00 a.m. yet."

Murphy didn't say anything, but just stared at Mitch. Cora tried to reason with him. "Maybe if you talked to Dad, he'd listen. He won't listen to any of us."

Mitch expelled his irritation in a long breath. "Why has this come as such a big surprise? Remember when Murphy told him his sidewalk was going to cave in if he didn't fix it? Did he listen? No. He waited until it did cave in, then thundered on about it for days."

Cora lifted her chin, an angry flush appearing on

her cheeks. "This isn't exactly somebody's sidewalk, Mitchell," she snapped in her snotty lawyer's tone. "This is about four people whose lives could be irrevocably altered if we don't do things by the book. If Dad stirs up a hornet's nest and they get kicked out, they will never get back in."

He hated it when she scored a point. Mitch heaved another sigh and mentally conceded, resigning himself to the inevitable. "Look, I will do what I can. But I don't have any more influence on him than you do. And I'm not sure doing things by the book is going to make a difference. It's not going to change anything as far as the Rodriguezes are concerned."

Murphy tipped his head to one side, an evil glint appearing in his eyes. "Well, there *is* one sure solution. Like Baba said, you could just marry her, bro," he stated, grinning broadly. "You'd probably have to convince Immigration that you guys were engaged before she got here. But hey, if she was married, then she would definitely meet all the requirements."

Mitch didn't even validate Murphy's asinine comments with an answer. "Help yourself to the coffee. I'm going for a shower."

They were gone when he returned to the kitchen twenty minutes later, but that didn't necessarily mean he was suddenly frustration free. Cora's perfume lingered, and he had developed a headache. He'd also gotten heartburn from his one joy in the morning—his first cup of coffee. Then two buttons came off his favorite shirt. Hell, he figured he should just scrap the morning before he even got started.

Mitch went downstairs, dread dogging every step.

The way his day had begun, it could only go downhill from there.

But instead, he found out a whole bunch of things had gone right. The Easter shipment had come in, and Doris had turned Maria loose on creating new baskets with that theme, which were spectacular. The place was as spotless as a garden center could get. And his staff was clearly glad to have him back, which picked up his spirits. But the really good news was that Doris had decided to showcase Maria's original baskets, and they had sold like hotcakes, even with the hiked prices.

Doris had the amount all tallied up, and Maria's share set aside in a brown envelope. She handed it and a tally sheet to Mitchell. He whistled when he saw the total. "Hey, not bad for stuff that was slated for the dump."

Doris grinned. "Hey yourself. If you think that was worth a whistle, wait until you see what she did with the *lilium longiflorum.*" She gave the envelope he was holding a little flip. "You give it to her, Boss. It'll give her a lift. She's been kinda down lately." She waggled her hand at Mitch. "And just a little touchy. So be nice."

He glared at Doris. "I'm always nice."

She patted his cheek and turned away. "Sure you are. And dogs don't bite."

Mitch gave her another glare and headed the other way. Women. Sometimes there was just no way of coming out on top. He tried to hang on to his annoyance, but the tally sheet and envelope practically burned his hand. He didn't want to be reminded of

Maria or her situation. Especially when he knew damned well how it was going to end.

He found her in the second greenhouse, up on a wobbly stepladder, winding long tendrils of jasmine through a high arch of latticework. His heart dropped about ten stories. Good God, that ladder was a wreck, and if it collapsed, she'd go right through the flimsy display. What in hell was she trying to do, kill herself? And who in hell had built the lattice arch, and where had all the jasmine plants come from? They certainly hadn't been there a week ago.

Muttering under his breath, he stomped over and grabbed the ladder. "Damn it, Maria. What do you think you're doing up there? That's why we have Abel hanging around eating doughnuts. Now get down before you break your neck."

She kept on carefully weaving the vines through the trellis. Her voice was that of an annoyed parent, as if prompting a spoiled child in the use of proper behavior. "Do not use that tone on me, Mitchell," she said, her own tone clear and precise. "You have very bad manners."

Maybe it was all the acidic coffee churning in his gut, but her patronizing tone ticked him right off. "Okay. Enough of the games. Now get down. I've got some business to discuss with you."

She acted if she hadn't heard a word he said. But he could tell from the angle of her chin that he had ticked *her* off. He didn't really care. She had no business being up an eight-foot ladder.

But did she listen? No. She just kept weaving the jasmine tendrils through the lattice, her chin stuck out a mile.

Clamping his temper down and his mouth shut, Mitch made a calm, rational decision to let her have her own way. She had been having a bad time, and he'd cut her a little slack this time.

The scent of bruised jasmine blossoms filled the air, and she tucked the last shoot in, then began straightening leaves. Straightening leaves, for Pete's sake!

Suddenly his resolution to keep his mouth shut went right down the toilet. "Maria..." he said, in a tone of voice that let her know she had pushed him as far as she could push him. Lifting her nose in the air, she came down the ladder. She brushed off her hands, then stiffly picked up two empty earthenware pots that were sitting on the floor. She was about to flounce off when he shoved the envelope and tally sheet at her. His tone was clipped and businesslike. "This is your share from the basket sales."

Her chin up, she took them and glanced at the tally sheet. She froze, as if he'd just poked her finger in a live socket. Then she jammed both the sheet and the envelope back in his hand. Her voice had an icy tone to it. "That is too much. I will not take that much."

She was about to stalk off but he caught her smock. His annoyance climbing a couple of notches, he stuffed the money and tally sheet in the big patch pocket on her garment. He couldn't quite keep the irritation out of his voice. "Take it, damn it. That was the deal. Fifty-fifty, and that's what you're getting. If you didn't like the arrangement, you should have said so."

She turned slowly, deliberately giving him a stare that would freeze boiling oil. "I *did* say so. But did you listen? No. You must have it your way."

Spots of temper stained her cheeks and she leaned over and angrily brushed some bits of peat moss off the wooden bunk that held flowering plants.

For some reason, her fussing pushed all of his buttons, and he jammed his hands on his hips. "Damn it, you don't have to *dust* in here, Maria. I don't expect it to be perfect."

She straightened and stiffened her spine, then faced him with that same slow deliberation. Her eyes flashing with temper, she stared at him. "You do not want perfect. I will give you not perfect." And she lifted her hands and dropped both pots from shoulder height, shards of pottery scattering everywhere.

Dumbfounded, Mitch stared at her, not quite believing what she had just done. With a tight, contemptuous smile, she whirled around and marched down the aisle, her back as straight and stiff as a board. Mitch stared after her, feeling as if someone had just pitched him out of a window. So that's all it took to detonate that fiery temper of hers. It was like watching fireworks go off. He found himself grinning, his cranky mood and headache suddenly gone.

So now he knew what happened when somebody tweaked Senora Rodriguez's nose. Very interesting. Very unpredictable. Very enlightening. When she let loose, she put on quite a show. Still grinning, he turned and headed toward the back storage area, whistling to himself. He guessed since he'd set her off, it was his responsibility to clean up after the explosion. He wondered how long it would take her to cool down.

He thought about the episode off and on all day, and every time it crossed his mind, he wanted to smile.

It must be quite a rush, to let go like that and let things fly. One thing for sure, it was quite the rush to watch.

Mitch kept an eye out for her the rest of the day, just to see how long it took her to get over her snit, but he didn't see hide nor hair of her. Either she was holed up somewhere, still steaming mad, or she was having an attack of the guilts. It wasn't until late afternoon, about the time she usually left, that he spotted her outside. She was sitting on a huge, flat rock down by the creek, huddled in her jacket, her knees drawn up and her arms wrapped around them.

It was a gorgeous day, with water running and real heat in the sunshine, and there was the indescribable smell of spring in the air. Mitch knew the ice had gone out of the creek—he'd heard it when he was out in the storage shed—but he wondered what had drawn her there. He was about to head out to the bank, but got as far as the door, then changed his mind. Instead, he went into the staff room and poured two cups of coffee, thinking about how to handle what had happened that morning. The last thing he wanted was for her to feel guilty. He wanted to make a joke out of it, if at all possible. But he didn't want to set her off again, either.

She was so deep in thought, he was at the rock before she heard him. Without giving her a chance to say anything, he grinned at her and handed her a mug of coffee. "I gotta tell you, I enjoyed the show."

She looked at him, clearly confused. "Pardon?"

Mitch made a throwing motion, then took a sip of coffee, watching her over the rim. He saw tints of embarrassment climb up her cheeks. It was all he

could do not to laugh. His expression completely sober, he lowered the cup and spoke, his tone thick with
amusement. "So tell me—what do you do for an en-
core, Ms. Rodriguez? You know, a repeat performance?"

She gave him a narrow look, a tiny glint of humor
appearing in her dark eyes. "You do not want to
know."

He chuckled and sat down on the rock beside her,
surprised at how warm it was. Stretching his legs out
in front of him, he took another sip and watched the
sunlight on the water.

"I am sorry, Mitchell," she said, her voice quiet
and subdued. "And thank you for cleaning up the broken pots."

"You don't have to apologize. I had it coming."

Smiling widely, he glanced at her, his heart missing
a beat when he saw the desolation in her eyes. He
might not have had a whole lot of experience with
personal defeat, but he could recognize the effects in
others. Looking away, he took another sip, then tried
to set off another spark. "So how come you're sitting
out here? Did you run out of things to smash inside?"

That got a small chuckle out of her, and she cupped
her hands around the mug. "No. I am waiting for
Cora. We are to meet with the immigration lawyer."

He caught the undercurrent of futility in the soft lilt
of her Spanish accent, and he forced himself to take
another sip. An idea had been cooking in his head ever
since Roberto had told him what they were doing with
the tips. But he had hesitated, partly because the idea
scared the hell out of him. Having her working for
him was bad enough; the prospect of her living across

the hall was downright terrifying. He didn't want anybody that close. Especially this woman.

Maria shivered and pulled her coat tighter around her, then wrapped her hands around her mug again, her somber gaze fixed on the bubbling creek. It was the shiver that did it—just her simple little shiver that broke down his resistance.

Feeling as if he had a bunch of birds suddenly beating around in his chest, he cleared his throat, then came at the proposition from the long way around. "When we built the garden center," he said, his tone surprisingly normal, "we designed it so there was space upstairs for a couple of apartments, as well as some additional office space. I live in one apartment, and the other one was for the first manager I had."

He took another sip of coffee to fortify himself, then continued. "I'm going to be doing more landscaping this year—a lot more, in fact. So I'll need someone else here—someone who's prepared to live on site and keep an eye on things at night. Preferably someone who knows the operation. I can't expect Doris to be here twelve or fourteen hours a day." His heartbeat accelerating, he screwed up his courage and finally looked at her. "I wondered if you might be interested."

She stared at him with a stunned expression, as if he'd just tossed her into the creek, but the pulse in her neck had gone into overdrive. Mitch laced his hands around his mug and looked away. "The apartment is only a two bedroom, but it is fully furnished, right down to dishes and linens." He glanced back, holding her stunned gaze, his muscles tense. For some reason he couldn't define, this was suddenly one fight he was determined to win. And he used a very dirty trick to make sure he did. "You do a good job, Maria, and you're dependable. And it would be helping me out a lot if you'd say yes."

A glimmer of tears immediately appeared in her eyes, and Mitch had to look away, experiencing such a thickness in his chest, he could barely swallow. The muscles in his face tight, he looked down at his half-empty cup, trying not to think how he would react if she said no.

There was a light touch on his arm, and he looked at her, his expression shuttered. She gazed at him a moment, then smiled a smile that reached right through to his heart. "You are not doing this to be kind?"

He wasn't sure why he was doing this, but it didn't have anything to do with being kind. He shook his head, his voice very gruff when he answered. "No."

A sparkle appeared in her eyes and her sweet, sweet smile broadened into a grin. "And I can break more pots when I am angry?"

It was as if she'd pulled a plug on the pressure in his chest, and he was able to respond with a genuine chuckle. "Just keep a record, okay?"

Maria held his gaze for a minute, then gave that familiar little shrug of hers and gazed out across the water. "I would be unfair to you, perhaps, if I say yes." She turned and met his gaze, her eyes dark with worry. "There could be problems with our application, Mitchell," she said softly. A look of panic appeared in her eyes, and she abruptly glanced away, her grip tightening on her mug. "We might not be allowed to stay."

He wanted to touch her, to give her some small gesture of comfort, but he didn't. Instead, he turned to stare across the water. "I know."

"If you want to… Let me think of the right word. If you want to *retract* your offer, I will understand, Mitchell."

Forcing a smile on his face, he looked back at her. "Nope. The offer stands. But I'll make sure the dishes in the apartment are unbreakable."

She laughed and dropped her head to her knees, shaking it in remorse. "Ah, Mitchell. Sometimes my temper—it is a wild thing. And sometimes it escapes me, and does what it wants."

It was the way she said it, as if she and her temper had been at odds for a long time, that struck him as really funny, and he laughed out loud. He gave her shoulder a little shove. "You can't fool me, Rodriguez. You and your temper get along just fine." Resisting the urge to ruffle her hair, he got up and dumped out the remainder of his coffee. "So. Are you taking the job?"

Even though her voice was muffled, he could tell she was smiling. "I am taking the job."

"Then come on. I'll show you the apartment."

He heard her scramble off the rock, then catch up to him. "So, Mitchell," she said, mimicking his speech pattern. "Are you so bossy always?"

He grinned and kept walking. Bossy, huh? He was going to have to talk to Doris about the vocabulary lessons.

He shot Maria an amused look. "Yeah, because I'm the boss."

It was an education all by itself, watching her inspect the apartment. She was like a little kid unwrapping presents, only with her it was a different kind of unwrapping. She opened every door to every cupboard and every closet, then clapped her hands together in delight when she discovered the treasures hidden within.

He'd saved the kitchen until last, probably because he considered it the best room in the apartment—lots of cupboards, great cooking and work space, sunny eating area that overlooked the tree-lined access road. Leaning back against the wide windowsill, Mitch crossed his ankles and folded his arms, watching her, amused by the look of barely contained excitement. She opened the cupboard where the dishes were stacked—several complete place settings with a pretty design. Carefully she took out a plate and held it in her hand as if it were the rarest of bone china.

She met his gaze, a look of unspeakable awe on her face. "I will take very good care, Mitchell," she said in a hushed tone. "I promise."

To be so awed by so little—what in hell kind of life had she had? A thick wad of emotion nailed him right in the chest, and it was all he could do to hold on to the smile. "I meant it when I said they were unbreakable."

She looked from him to the plate, then back at him, a mischievous glint appearing in her eyes. She shifted her hold, and for an instant, he thought she was going to drop it just to challenge him. He was almost sorry when she didn't. As if aware that he had correctly read her, she lifted one shoulder and blushed, then carefully placed the plate back on top of the others. "It is beautiful, Mitchell, your apartment."

"It's now *your* apartment, Maria," he said firmly, not wanting her to feel indebted in any way, shape or form. "It comes with the job."

"Oh, look," she exclaimed, opening the large, custom-made drawer for the pots and pans. "Cookware!"

He shook his head and grinned. Not one of his sisters would have been at all delighted over pots and pans. And then a question popped out without him even thinking about it. "How old were you when you got married?"

She glanced at him, a lid in her hand. "Nearly seventeen."

"So the boys were little more than babies."

"*Sí*," she responded, totally engrossed in checking out the latest find. "Roberto was almost two. And Enrico was a little baby. The wife of Pedro—ah," she muttered, catching this mistake. "Pedro's wife had died, and he needed a mother for his babies." She looked up, having no idea the effect her offhand comment had on Mitch. "He was a good man, Pedro. And kind. We did not have much money, but we had a good life." Her eyes clouded over, and Mitch could almost hear her mental addendum—*until he got sick.* Needing to erase that look from her eyes, he shifted his position, and reached over to open the casement window. "Here, check this out. See what you think of the view."

She came over to stand beside him, and he suddenly wished she didn't smell like the shipment of gardenias that had arrived that morning. Then he noticed the smear of bright yellow pollen on the swell of one breast, and he had to close his eyes and fight for air as his heartbeat faltered.

Getting a grip, he moved away, clenching his hands into fists as he forced himself to regulate his breathing, the scent of gardenias following him.

Too close. He had let her get too close.

But a little voice in his head disputed that. No, it said, not close enough. Not nearly close enough.

Chapter 5

He knew almost immediately he had made a mistake. He should have known better. You didn't go jumping into the deep end without thinking, and you didn't make a decision on the spur of the moment. But he had. And now the Rodriguezes were living across the hall, and he was going to have to deal with the consequences.

He probably could have gotten a handle on it, but the lingering scent of gardenias seemed to be everywhere. And so was she. Both the scent of gardenias and one Maria Rodriguez started turning up in his dreams. On top of all that, he had this feeling that she never slept. Within hours of her moving in, he also had the sneaky feeling that she was the one who was running the whole show, not him.

But what had caught him totally off guard was that within two days of her moving in, they developed this goofy kind of rapport. It started almost immediately, the morning of the second day. By a stroke of pure coincidence, they had both opened the doors leading to the common hallway at the exact same time. She gave him a wide-eyed, frazzled look, trying to stuff her arm into her smock, which was inside out. With her hair sticking out as if she had just yanked her sweater on over her head, she stared at him a split second, then slammed her door shut.

Curious to see how she was going to get out of this one, he leaned against the wall and waited. She finally opened the door, her hair back and under control in a neat twist. Her smock was on right side out and properly done up, and she had arranged her expression into one of absolute composure. Acting as if she hadn't seen him thirty seconds before, she greeted him. "Good morning, Mitchell."

He kept his voice very solemn. "Good morning, Maria." He was going to let the first encounter slide by, but there was something about the angle of her chin that he couldn't ignore. He just had to bait her. "Just so you know," he said, his tone deliberately benevolent, "there's a crazy woman in your apartment, fighting to get out."

Her chin came up a little higher, and a flush crept up her cheeks.

He gave her shoulder a little bump. "Slept in, huh?"

She slanted a pointed look at him as he opened the fire door at the end of hall and held it for her. "I did not sleep *in*. I overslept," she corrected, with that regal tone of hers.

He somehow managed to keep a straight face, his

expression solemn. "I apologize. I didn't know there was a difference."

She gave his shoulder a shove, a glint appearing in her eyes. "You are making fun of me, no?"

"I would never make fun of you, Maria."

Before he realized her intent, she jabbed him in the ribs, right where he was most vulnerable, and he immediately let go a huff and caved in. She raised her eyebrows, then lifted her finger to her mouth and blew on it, as if it were a smoking gun. Then she gave him a big smirk. "Ha. I win."

So, she thought that stunt was pretty cute. He wouldn't let her know it, but he actually thought it was pretty cute, too.

Later in the morning, he was heading through the garden center with a spray bottle in his hand, on his way to mist the plants in the display area in the front window. He caught a glimpse of her down one aisle, her back to him as she refilled the bird seed display.

Although he had never been one for pranks or practical jokes, this was one opportunity that was just too good to miss. Changing the setting to "stream," he came up quietly behind her and spoke her name. She turned, and he shot her in the chest. He gave her an equally big smirk. "Now *I* win."

She let out a yell in Spanish as the cold water hit her, then started laughing. Mopping her chest with a dust cloth, she fixed him with an evil eye. "You, Mitchell. You are a bad one."

The water had splashed her face, and there were drops on one cheek and across her nose. He stuck his free hand in his pocket to keep from wiping it away. Trying to keep it light, he did a gunslinger flip with the spray bottle, then sauntered off. "God, but I'm good."

She was still laughing. "No. You are bad. Very bad."

It wasn't as if she was all sweetness and light, though. He hadn't known he was even capable of arguing the way he argued with her. Everything was a big debate. If he wanted something done one way, she would argue about doing it another. And she would really get rolling—in English. Half the time, he really didn't care one way or the other; it was just that if he was in the mood, it was kind of interesting to push her buttons and watch the sparks fly. Then he would make a big production of moving anything breakable out of her reach. That really steamed her. And it made him smile just thinking about it.

But with Easter coming up, he didn't have time to think about much of anything. With all the hard-core gardeners out browsing, the center was nuts.

By Friday night, Mitch was running on empty, and all he wanted to do was go upstairs and lock himself in his apartment, have a cold beer and stare at a blank wall. But twenty minutes before closing time, Mrs. Van Bueren showed up, and he knew he could kiss his cold beer goodbye.

Mrs. V.B., as Doris called her, was a very wealthy widow, and every Easter she bought potted plants for every single person in the seniors' lodge where her ninety-year-old mother lived. It wasn't as if she was a witch and hard to deal with; she was actually a very sweet, kindhearted woman and generous to a fault. But she could take longer making a decision on what to buy than any other person on the face of the earth.

Mitch wasn't sure the word *decision* was even in her vocabulary. Faced with a choice, the woman simply could not make up her mind, and multiplying that by fifty-five, he knew he could still be there when the sun came up.

Mitch tried to drag up some enthusiasm for the process. He truly did like the woman, and she had a heart as big as all outdoors. And he certainly valued her loyalty and her considerable business. He just didn't want her business tonight. Tomorrow, he would have welcomed her with open arms. Tonight he wanted to bang his head against the wall.

He was in the greenhouse with her, nearly blind with exhaustion, picking up plants and putting them back, when Maria swept in. She stopped abruptly, her expression startled, as if she didn't expect to find anyone there. Probably because Doris had turned on the Closed sign, locked the doors and sent everyone else home at least half an hour ago.

It took Maria about thirty seconds, eyeing the big trolley with only three plants on it, to figure out what was going on. A warm smile on her face, she came over and touched Mrs. V.B. on the arm. "It is hard to choose, is it not?"

Mrs. V.B. gave her an anxious, apologetic look. "I have such an awful time making up my mind."

With that same kindness she showed the seniors, she patted the older woman's arm. "Then I will help you. Tell me what you are wanting."

Mrs. V.B. told her, and Maria listened intently, nodding her head. When the customer finished, Maria gave her a bright smile. "Well, I have the most perfect thing for you. Come. I will show you."

His feeling of exhaustion giving way to plain old curiosity, Mitch followed in their wake, wondering how Miss Maria was going to pull this rabbit out of the bag.

She did it in ten minutes. "See these pots with the shoots coming up? They are a mixture of spring bulbs. And they will be perfect. In a few days, maybe five, the buds will open, and there will be beautiful blossoms. And if your friends wish, they can keep them to plant outside."

Mrs. Van Bueren's face lit up with a delighted smile. "Well, then. I'll take fifty-five."

Mitch nearly fell over in a dead faint. A decision. A crisp, no-nonsense decision, just like that.

By the time they made arrangements for delivery and had settled the bill, it was nearly ten o'clock. Not wanting her out in the parking lot alone, Mitch walked the wealthy matron to her car and made sure she got off safely. Then he went back to the garden center, fatigue piling in on him. All he wanted to do was go to bed.

But Maria had other ideas. She met him at the door and literally bullied him into the second greenhouse, insisting that she had a surprise for him.

It was a surprise, all right. She had dragged some garden furniture into the middle of a group of tall tropical plants, and even had a huge canvas umbrella fixed in the table. The fountain was running, and there was a small shopping bag sitting on the wrought iron table. She lined him up with the chair, then pushed him down into it.

He chuckled and shook his head, and she waggled her finger at him. "Not to laugh, Mitchell," she scolded. "This is not funny. This is very serious business." Whipping a cloth napkin out of the bag, she dropped it across his lap and put her hands on her hips. "Tonight, I give you lessons, Mitchell." Then she lifted out a dish full of lime wedges and a saltshaker. "Tonight, Mitchell Munroe, I teach you how to drink tequila."

He tipped his head back and laughed, and she sat down on the other side of the small table, then lifted a bottle of tequila and two shot glasses out of the bag. Her eyes dancing, she twisted off the top. "Have you ever..." she paused, and he could almost see her conjugating the verb in her head "...drunk tequila?"

Expelling the last of his laughter, he shook his head. "Nope, I'm a Scotch kinda guy."

She gave a dismissive sniff. "Scotch. A drink for babies." She filled the shot glasses, then showed him how to place the salt on the side of his fist. And she told him the drill: lick the salt, bash back the tequila and suck the lime.

After one shot and the ensuing kick, Mitch immediately understood what Maria was talking about. This was definitely not a drink for babies.

She kept egging him on, and pretty soon, they couldn't stop laughing. And by the time they polished off the bottle, the roof could have fallen in on him, and he couldn't have cared less.

Mitch was prepared to sleep in the lounge chair, but she wouldn't have any of that. Somehow, she managed to get him upstairs into his apartment, keeping him on his feet until she had him lined up with his bed. Then she let him go. Everything had gotten pretty fuzzy around the edges, and his mouth didn't want to work.

But one thing for sure, the lady could definitely slam 'em back.

And that was his last conscious thought.

When he came to the next morning, bright sunshine was streaming through the window. His mouth felt as if something had molted and made a nest in it, and he was not too anxious to move his head. Hell, he hadn't done anything that stupid in years.

Bracing himself for one hell of a hangover headache, he slowly got out of bed, waiting for the agony to strike. But nothing happened.

He got up and moved around, amazed that he wasn't blind with pain. But there was no pain. In fact, he felt pretty damned good. It was as if he'd done nothing more than have a good night's sleep. Squinting his eyes, he glanced at his watch. Nah. That couldn't be right. It couldn't be 12:30 p.m. He turned to check his clock radio, and yep, it said 12:30 p.m., too. No wonder he felt as if he'd had a good night's sleep. He'd been out cold for at least ten hours. And he couldn't remember the last time he'd slept ten hours in a stretch. Hell, maybe never.

He had a shower and went downstairs, bracing himself for a very hard time from Doris and the rest of the staff. Of course, the very first person he ran into was Maria. She flashed her dimples, winked at him, then pretended to bash back a shot of booze. Then raising her arms, she snapped her fingers in a gesture of victory. "Ha, Munroe. I win again."

He didn't laugh, but he wanted to. God, he wanted to. Just then Doris came around the corner and called out, "Oh, look, everybody. Grumpy just crawled out of his cave."

Mitch gave her a quelling look. "I have not been grumpy."

She and Maria exchanged long speaking looks, as if they were dealing with an odious child.

He shook his head, withholding a retort. Nothing like everybody ganging up on the boss. He pointed his finger at Maria. "I'll get you for this, Rodriguez. So watch your back."

She gave him a sassy little wiggle and a very sassy smile. "I do not think so, Munroe."

Lucky for him, he had a bunch of business to conduct out of the store, and he was gone most of the afternoon. And on the way home, he had to stop and get his van washed. The weather was holding, and the remaining snow was melting at such a rate the streets were nothing but slop. But he knew that if it kept up like this, within two days all the snow would be gone, except maybe in the heavy bush. Yep. Spring was definitely here. Excluding, of course, that last spring blizzard that invariably hit.

It was just going on three when he arrived back at the garden center. Doris must have seen him coming, because she met him at the door, a very worried look on her face. She grabbed his arm and steered him into one of the wide aisles. "You've gotta talk to Maria, Boss."

Stripping off his denim jacket, he frowned at her. "Why? What's wrong?"

Doris wrung her hands together. "That immigration lawyer stopped by about an hour ago, and she looked like hell after he left." As if realizing how she was fussing with the sleeve of his jacket, she stuck her hands in the patch pockets on her smock, her eyes dark with anxiety. "I tried to talk to her, but she just gave me that stiff little smile she sticks on when she's upset. She said nothing was wrong, but she's been holed up in the potting shed ever since."

Mitch handed his jacket to her, his face suddenly feeling very wooden. "Here. Toss this behind the counter for me."

Doris nodded and Mitch headed toward the shed, trying to ignore the crazy flutter in his belly. He wasn't getting involved. He was smarter than that. But they had become drinking buddies, damn it.

He did find her in the potting shed. She had a bunch of runt plants set out on the waist-high table and was methodically transplanting them into an earthenware bowl.

The room smelled of peat moss and damp potting soil, and dust motes climbed up the broad beam of light coming from the two large windows. The floor was worn planks, and she must have heard him enter, but she didn't even acknowledge his presence.

Sensing she did not want her immediate space invaded, he stopped by one of the thick wooden support pillars and, bracing one hand on the beam, rested the other hand on his hip. He considered her for a moment, then spoke, his tone quiet. "So do you want to tell me what happened this afternoon?"

She didn't even look up; she just kept transplanting. "Nothing happened this afternoon."

Mitch continued to study her, trying to figure out how to get her to open up. The only way he knew how was to hit below the belt. "I thought we were friends, Maria. You don't shut your friends out."

His gamble worked and Maria looked up him, her eyes brimming with misery, her face etched with strain. For a moment, he thought she'd actually break down, but she didn't. "You are my friend, Mitchell," she whispered unevenly. "But there is nothing you can do."

His own expression somber, he held her gaze. "Let me decide. Just tell me what happened."

She stared at him for a second, then she looked down and kept working with the plants. "Mr. Peterson came today—he is the immigration lawyer." She paused and shook her head, her voice breaking. "I—I cannot tell you this."

It was all he could do to stay right where he was. "Yes, you can, Maria," he said, his tone firm. "You have to tell someone."

She looked at him, so much sorrow in her eyes that it made his entire chest tighten up, and he gripped the support post. For a moment, he thought she wasn't going to respond, but finally she drew a deep, unsteady breath and looked down again. "I do not want to betray your father and mother, Mitchell."

Feeling as if his jaw was about to shatter, Mitch forced himself to relax the muscles in his face. "You aren't betraying anybody."

Without looking at him, she gave a defeated shrug. "Your parents were not happy with what Mr. Peterson told them, so they went to talk to your Immigration people. And now Mr. Peterson thinks perhaps the situation has been made worse."

Clenching his jaw, Mitch closed his eyes, a sick

feeling radiating through him. Damn it all to hell. Cora
and Murphy had warned him right after he got back
from the farm, and he had tried to talk to his old man.
But his mother, his ever-optimistic mother, was all for
going to talk directly to Immigration. She was absolutely convinced that all it would take was to find a
bureaucrat with an understanding heart. Mitch knew
the mind-set of bureaucracy, especially civil servants,
and he figured that finding someone in Immigration
with a heart was about as likely as finding a Revenue
Canada agent with a soul.

And now they had gone ahead and done it. Which
meant the fat was really in the fire.

Releasing a heavy sigh, he opened his eyes and
looked at her. What the hell could he say? He couldn't
tell her everything would be okay. Because it wasn't.
But maybe he could distract her.

He forced a smile onto his face. "Maybe it's time
for another tequila lesson."

That got an uneven chuckle out of her, and he saw
her quickly wipe her eyes. She tried to hang on to her
smile when she met his gaze, but her unhappiness won
out. Even from a distance, he caught the glimmer of
more tears, and there was a heartbreaking look in her
eyes. "I would be a good citizen, Mitchell. And my
boys would be good citizens also."

For one split second, his feet developed minds of
their own, and they wanted to march him right over
to her. But he anchored his wayward feet to the floor,
knowing he didn't dare breach his safety zone. He had
to do something, though, to wipe that grief-stricken
look off her face. And he had no idea where the in-

spiration came from. "Have you ever been ice skating?"

He had caught her totally off guard, and she looked at him as if he'd lost his mind. "No."

Feeling as if he'd accomplished something big by erasing that awful expression in her eyes, he crossed the room and grasped her wrist. "Well, then. It's time you did."

She tried to put on the brakes, but he simply dragged her. "But, Mitchell," she protested. "The plants."

"To hell with the plants. We're going skating."

Intent on taking her mind off her worries, he put any thoughts of her immigration problems out of his mind.

The trip to the rink was an experience he wasn't about to forget in the next fifty years. They'd borrowed his mother's skates, which were two sizes too big, and Maria thought it was the most bizarre thing that they were going to skate indoors. She only wiped out really badly ten or twelve times, but that was because she wouldn't let him help her. Not Miss Independence. She had to do it on her own. By the end of an hour, she was doing pretty darned good for a raw beginner, and there wasn't a trace of a shadow in her eyes. He didn't go in when they dropped off the skates at his parents', because he knew he'd get into one hell of an argument with his father if he did. And it was too late for arguing. The damage had already been done.

But thoughts of Maria came back with a vengeance in the middle of the night. Mitch had wakened from a disturbingly erotic dream, one that was so real, he half expected to find her in bed beside him. One that left him hard and aching, and his heart racing.

Mitchell was not at all happy about that dream— but he assured himself it meant nothing. It was some sort of weird lapse, an unconscious breakdown. It was just a damned dream. But the hard, cold reality of her situation was no dream, and he got such a sick flutter in his chest, it was as close to a panic attack as he ever wanted to get. And he knew he had to find a way to disconnect from both the dream and the reality.

It was 4:00 a.m., and he was so wide-awake and wound up that he was ready to chew nails. What he wanted to do was go outside and move about three truckloads of potting soil until he was so numb with exhaustion, he couldn't even think.

But he didn't have three truckloads of potting soil. So he did the next-best mind-numbing thing, and got up, went into his office and took care of every single piece of paper he could lay his hands on.

That ruse worked for one night, but he had a repeat dream about Maria the following night, and it was so hot, so erotic and so real that he finally ended up going for an hour-long run. But that only burned off that high-pitched edgy feeling; it didn't stop him from thinking. Try as he might, he could not get her face out of his mind. And it didn't help, knowing she was just across the hall. That didn't help at all.

Unable to face anyone, he took off for his tree farm again the next day. With his site manager there permanently, Mitch couldn't find a whole lot to do except some spring pruning. But after spending a day outside in the sun and fresh air, he felt a little calmer. At least that's what he told himself.

He convinced himself he had it together by the time he got back to the center late that night. But when he did his usual late-night check on the greenhouses, all he could smell were gardenias.

He didn't even try to sleep that night—he just couldn't risk it. So he spent all night pacing and putting up safe little compartments in his mind. It was just some sort of mental glitch, these crazy dreams. And if he really focused, he could compartmentalize them, too. Hell, that was how he'd survived all these years. Stuffing all that emotional stuff away in dark little holes. Damn it, he had done it before; he could do it again.

By sunup, he was so damned tired and had such a headache, he felt as if he'd been dropped on his head. He considered playing hooky, but they were going to have to start consolidating inventory to make room for the spring shipments that would start rolling in any day.

He was on the Bobcat, moving some pallets of interlocking bricks into the outside sales area, when Doris came tearing out, looking as if demons were after her. She yelled at him, and he put the Bobcat in neutral, wondering what had set her off this time.

By the time she reached him, she was out of breath and gasping for air. "You gotta come in, Boss. There's a guy in there who looks like a weasel." She closed her eyes and pressed her hand to her breast, fighting to catch her breath. Then she looked at him, fear in her eyes. "He's from Immigration, and he's looking for Maria. I told him I'd see if I could find her.''

Alarm making his gut knot, he shut off the Bobcat and climbed off. ''Where is she?''

''I think she's in the big greenhouse—in that back part where we store the extra stock of bedding plants.''

Mitch was off and running before Doris finished. His heart pounding, he shoved open the back door of the big greenhouse, a weird feeling of weakness rushing through him when he saw her. She and Roberto were busy clearing off the wooden bunks. There were only the two of them, and she was humming to herself. And not a weasel in sight. He hadn't had time to formulate a plan. All he knew was that he had to get her out of there.

But he was ten seconds too late. He reached her and had grasped her by the shoulder just as a man in a suit came around the corner. Putting his arm around her and pulling her against him, he swore under his breath. Great. Now they were dead twice over. Not only was she now under scrutiny from the feds, she was also clearly working. And Doris had been right. The man had weasel eyes and a ferret face, and Baba had taught her grandchildren well on what to expect from people with weasel eyes. Mitch detested him on sight. Damn it all to hell. In a protective gesture, he locked Maria against his side and wiped his face clear of any expression.

Maria looked up at him, and he could tell by the glimmer of fear in her eyes and her grip on the back of his shirt that she had put the whole show together. As if sensing danger, Roberto came to stand on the other side of Mitch, his body stiff and erect.

Deciding that a strong offense was the better part of defense, Mitch gave Maria a reassuring squeeze. He spoke, his tone clipped with anger. "My manager tells me you're from Immigration. So what are you doing here?"

The man set his briefcase on one of the shelves on the tier, then gave Mitch a chilly smile. "I'm here to inform Mrs. Rodriguez—" he gave Maria an insolent nod "—that she will be allowed to stay in Canada until her ninety-day visitor allocation has expired, then she will be asked to leave. She will not be allowed to apply for landed immigrant status. According to our records, she entered Canada on February 25. We expect her to depart on or before May 24."

He shoved a business card into Mitch's hand, and Mitch felt Maria sag against him. Maybe it was the weight of her defeat. Maybe it was the stricken look in Roberto's eyes. And maybe it was because he hated arrogant bastards who used their position to bully people. Whatever the reason, a cold fury like he'd never known coursed through Mitch, and right behind it, a hardened resolve. No way. No damned way.

Grasping Maria by the back of the head, he dragged her around and jammed her face into his chest, making it impossible for her to speak. And he jumped in with both feet, his tone like cold steel. "I don't know where you got your information…" he paused, checking the card "…Mr. Felder. But Mrs. Rodriguez isn't going anywhere." An instant recall flashed in his mind, of what Murphy had said—about them needing to be already engaged.

His voice still hard, Mitch forged on. "We've been engaged for over a year, we're living under the same

roof and we are getting married in ten days.'' Maria
went stiff and tried to break away, but he gripped her
head and wrapped his other arm around her, locking
her against him in an unbreakable hold. Damn. She
was a helluva lot stronger than she looked. In spite of
how bloody furious he was, he wanted to laugh. Trying to make out as if he were simply comforting her,
he glared at Mr. Felder. ''So you can march all your
paperwork right back to wherever it came from, because my wife will be staying in Canada.''

Mr. Felder sniffed, then gave him a nasty little
smirk. ''How convenient.''

Mitch mentally scrambled, then came up with the
offer of hard evidence. ''Well, tell you what. How
about I supply you with records of my family's long
association with Mrs. Rodgriguez? And how about I
supply you with copies of airline tickets when I flew
to Mexico to visit? Then we can talk about convenient.
I can put it all in writing, and I can provide all the
documentation.''

Maria went dead still in his arms, and he could almost hear the wheels grinding away in her head. It
wasn't an out-and-out lie. He had gone south several
times in the past couple of years, trips to meet with
various producers, every time on business. But Mr.
Felder would never be able to prove it.

Roberto moved closer so he stood shoulder to shoulder with Mitch. ''Is true,'' he said, looking as honest
and sincere as anyone who was lying could look.
Mitch winked at him, and Roberto winked back. Mitch
wasn't sure if it was her Latin temper breaking loose,
or if she was fighting suffocation, but Maria twisted
in his arms and bit him. Wanting to swear and grin at

the same time, he trapped her arm so she couldn't get loose and made a phony comforting sound, pressing his mouth to her hair. She went instantly still. He half expected her to kick him in the shins.

Felder at least had the decency to look flustered. "Well, your parents should have mentioned that. That puts the application in a completely different light."

Mitch knew they weren't out of the woods yet, and he played it out to the bitter end. He used the same tone of voice on Felder that Maria had once used on him, as if he were speaking to a very slow child. "My parents aren't exactly in the picture, Mr. Felder. I wanted Maria to have a chance to spend some time here, to see if she liked it, before we made a decision. So my *parents* don't know yet."

Roberto shifted his stance, looking like a young, cocky matador. "But I know."

It was all Mitch could do not to laugh. What a ham. Roberto looked at him, an unholy glint in his eyes. Mitch met his gaze, a small smile sneaking out. He knew he had good reason to like this kid.

As if suspecting he'd been had but not entirely sure, Felder snapped up his briefcase and gave Mitch a chilly look. "We will be in touch."

He disappeared and Mitch looked at Roberto, indicating the door with his chin. "Keep an eye out, will you? Your mother and I are going to have a little talk."

Roberto grinned at him. "I will watch with both eyes, Mitchell."

Mitch gave him a lopsided grin. "Very funny, kid."

Knowing he was going to have a tiger by the tail the minute he let her go, Mitch got a firm hold on

Maria's wrist, then, before she could really catch her balance, hauled her outside. As soon as she got some purchase in the gravel, she tried to break free. "Let me go, Mitchell," she snapped, her tone laced with pure temper.

Amusement percolating through him, he kept walking. "Nope. We're going to the creek. Then we're going to sit down and have a talk."

She tried to twist her wrist free. "I will not sit down with you, and I will not talk."

Glad she couldn't see his face, Mitch grinned. Lord, but she was a spitfire. "Fine. Then you can listen."

Finally realizing that there was no way she could win the tug-of-war against someone his size, Maria stuck her chin in the air and marched alongside him, looking straight ahead. Familiar with that stubborn look, he did not loosen his grip.

When they reached the big flat rock, Mitch stopped walking and looked at her. "If I let go of you, will you sit down and listen to what I have to say?"

She didn't answer. She just glared at him.

"Fine," he said. "Then we'll do it your way."

Knowing she didn't have anything to negotiate with, she rolled her eyes in annoyance, her eyes still flashing fire. "I will listen," she said, a warning tone in her voice. "But then you will listen, Mitchell. I have much to say to you."

He let go of her and she jerked her arm away, her back rigid with indignation. She sat on the rock and glared at him. "So speak."

After considering her a moment, he finally did. "Do you want your boys to stay in Canada? Do *you* want to stay here?" he asked, his tone even.

He could tell from the way she looked at him that she hadn't expected him to lay that on her, and she stared back. Finally she threw up her hands and made an exasperated sound. "Of course we want to be allowed to stay in Canada. But—"

He held up one finger. "No buts, Maria. The deal was I talk, then you talk."

She folded her arms and narrowed her eyes at him. "Fine," she snapped.

Resting his hands on his hips, he stared down at the ground, assembling his thoughts. He had never in his wildest dreams considered marriage a viable option, but here he was. What had sounded like total insanity a couple of weeks ago now sounded absolutely rational. And he was a rational man. If staying here was what she really wanted, between the two of them they could pull this whole thing together. Now all he had to do was come up with a straightforward, rational, logical argument. Although from past experience, he wasn't too sure it was a concept she was familiar with. Exhaling, he prepared himself.

"Look," he said, meeting her gaze. "I just acted on the spur of the moment there."

A strange look flitted across her face, and the rigidity left her body. It was kind of like watching air leak out of a balloon, and he realized she thought he was backing out. She didn't look all that happy about it, which made him feel a whole lot better for some reason.

Bracing one foot on the rock beside her, he rested both arms on his thigh, fixing his gaze on her. "We could make it work, Maria. You'd like to see the boys have a chance. I think they're great kids, and I know

I'd like to see them have a chance. What's wrong with that? You're unattached. I'm unattached. I need someone to help me out here. You need a place to live. And by the sounds of it, getting married is your only option.''

An odd sense of purpose formed in his mind, and he locked his gaze on her. ''We can strike a deal. We can have a quiet ceremony, and we can stay married until you clear the immigration requirements, then we can go our separate ways. But whatever deal we strike, I really think we could pull this off. It isn't going to affect anyone else. It's just between you and me.''

The fire had gone out of her, but she was watching him with an assessing gaze, and he knew from her expression that there was a whole lot going on in her head. He just hoped she didn't turn this into another battle of wills.

Finally she looked down and picked at a loose thread on the front of her smock. ''But it would affect others, Mitchell. It would be an insult to your wonderful parents. And to your wonderful family.'' She looked up at him, her expression so serious that her eyes appeared almost black. Her tone was almost chastising when she continued. ''I do not think you know what a wonderful family you have, Mitchell.'' She looked away, then finally looked back at him. ''And I do not want them to think that I used their kindness and goodwill. I do not want them to think I used you. That would be such disrespect.''

Which put Mitch between a rock and a hard place. He didn't want her to think the family had been conniving behind her back. But he also wanted to be on the level with her. He shrugged and gave her a small smile. "Do you honestly think it hasn't crossed their minds, Maria? My grandmother has been dropping broad hints ever since you arrived, and my family would do almost anything so you could stay." *Even marry you off to me,* he thought, a twist of humor surfacing. But he couldn't exactly tell her that. His expression carefully arranged, he met her gaze dead on. "But if we do this, we have to be careful that we don't give the game away as far as Immigration is concerned."

She swallowed hard and twisted her hands together, her gaze dark and worried. "It is not just your family, Mitchell. It is a big decision."

Feeling as if he were standing on the edge of a very high precipice, Mitch straightened and turned away. He hooked his thumbs in the front pockets of his jeans and stared across the creek, not liking the feeling in his gut. How could he get her to see the simple common sense of the plan? He frowned, trying to think of all the things that might hold her back.

Playing out a sudden hunch, he turned. The explanation had to come from her; it simply wouldn't work if he put words in her mouth. So he fixed his attention on her, his gaze steady. "What else, Maria? What else is bothering you?"

She met his eyes, then looked away and rolled her palms out in a helpless gesture. Crouching down in front of her, he hooked a knuckle under her chin, prompting her to look at him. "Tell me," he said softly.

She repeated the gesture. "It is the church," she whispered. "Marriage should not be used to deceive. Marriage is to sanctify."

Mitch released his hold on her face, then caught both of her hands between his. He gave her an encouraging smile. "There have been arranged marriages for hundreds of years, and there will continue to be arranged marriages for hundreds more." He softened his tone even more, not wanting to wound in any way. "Wasn't your marriage with Pedro basically arranged by the priest? Didn't he bring you two together? So what would be so wrong about us having an arranged marriage here?" He tightened his grip on her hands. "Look. I need something from you. You need something from me. And if you're that worried about what my parents will think, we don't need to explain anything. In fact, I'd probably prefer it that way."

Her expression fixed with uncertainty, she swallowed hard. "You do not think this is wrong?"

He smiled at her and gave her hands a little shake. "No. I don't think it's wrong. I think it's right. It's right for you. It's right for the boys. And it works for me."

Maria stared at him, processing, thinking; then she drew a deep breath and looked away. "If I do this, if we do this arrangement, I do not think we should sleep together."

Mitch got such an unexpected jolt, it derailed his entire thought processes. Okay, it had crossed his mind on occasion. And it had certainly been real in those damned dreams—but it hadn't crossed his mind as part of the deal. He wasn't that much of an opportunist. His tone was gruff when he answered, "If that's what you want, fine."

She abruptly turned one hand within his grasp and

clutched him, as if she, too, felt as if they were standing on the edge of a steep precipice. Her eyes dark with anxiety, she stared up at him and hung on for dear life. He smiled at her and tightened his hold on her hand, silently reassuring her. "Stay, Maria."

She started to tremble, and she closed her eyes and rested her forehead against his. "If we do this," she whispered unevenly, "we must do it in a way that will not upset your parents or harm my sons. You must promise me."

She was close—so close—that he could feel her warm breath on their joined hands. The scent of gardenias filled his senses, and as he closed his eyes and hung on to her hands, a dizzy feeling fizzled through him, a feeling he had never experienced before. It left him weak. It left him light-headed. It was like breathing pure oxygen. Like soaring. Like experiencing the rarest form of flight.

The warmth of her breath radiated through him, pumping through his entire system. He tightened his hold on her hands in unspoken assurance and swallowed hard, his own voice unsteady. "I promise."

Chapter 6

It was weird. After they struck their agreement, Mitch could hardly stand to have her out of his sight. He told himself he felt that way because he could see it in her face—that if she spent too much time alone, she'd start second-guessing the deal. It was as if all her doubts and fears would pile in on her, and the reality would throw her into an absolute panic.

But she was okay when she was with him—in fact, his presence obviously reassured her, so he made damned sure he stuck pretty close. Granted, there were moments when he wondered why he'd fought so hard to persuade her to go along with his crazy scheme. It really didn't matter one way or the other to him. At least he kept telling himself it didn't.

But since she was still a little skittish, Mitch figured it was best if he gave her some time to really get used to the idea. So he suggested they not say anything to anyone until after the Easter rush at work was over.

Maria seemed almost giddy with relief, and she never even argued with him—not one little bit—when he suggested that it might be best if they leveled with the boys. Especially when Roberto had been there when the plot had been hatched. The kid was no dummy, and Mitch wanted to be direct and to the point with both him and Enrico. He didn't really care about making any kind of explanation to anyone else except Murphy, and he didn't want any of them—the two boys or his brother—laboring under any false expectations.

And out of respect for Maria and her beliefs, he decided to go to Mass with the Rodriguez family on Easter Sunday. From different comments, he knew they attended Mass regularly, and he knew it was important to her. So important that he hadn't even suggested they make their merger before a priest. He didn't want her worrying about that, too.

His going to church with them raised a few eyebrows in his family. Which ticked him off. It wasn't as if he had never been to Mass before. Jessica had turned Catholic when she and Marco got married, and Mitch had attended every single one of the baptisms and first communions of her kids. So the rites and pageantry were all familiar, but what caught him off guard was how natural it felt being there with her, as if it were a normal part of their everyday life. That made him just a little uneasy, as if part of him knew something the rest of him didn't.

Going to church was easy. Telling his parents was not going to be so easy. He knew Maria was dreading

it, and there was no way he was going to make her
run that gauntlet. Not in a million years.

So one night, when he knew his parents were going
to be home alone, he went over and told them that he
and Maria were getting married—that they were not
going to make a big deal out of it, that they were
simply going to go to the Justice of the Peace. His
parents were ecstatic, and if he hadn't known better,
he would have sworn they had never even heard
Baba's repeated suggestions that Mitch should marry
her. The way they acted, it was the real thing. Mitch
would have bet his socks that his mother was on the
phone to the rest of his siblings the minute he walked
out the door.

After leaving his parents, he went directly to Murphy's. He didn't want Murphy to get the wrong idea.
And his brother wasn't quite so thickheaded; he got
the picture.

When Mitch dropped the goods on him, Murphy
was sitting in his big leather chair, his arms resting on
his thighs. He looked up at his brother, his expression
sober. "Are you okay with this, bro? Or did we pressure you into it?"

Feeling as if he'd been put through the wringer by
his parents, Mitch dragged his hand wearily down his
face, then met his brother's sober gaze. "I'm okay
with it." He tipped his head back against the cushy
padding in the big easy chair he was sitting in and
stared at the ceiling for a minute. Then he looked at
his brother again. "Do me a favor, will you?"

His expression unsmiling, Murphy nodded. "Name
it."

"Just don't let them turn this into a three-ring circus, all right? We want to keep it simple."

Murphy gave him a lopsided smile. "Hell, why don't you just ask me to go move a mountain? You know this family doesn't know the meaning of simple." Mitch gave him a long, weary look, and Murphy grinned. "But I'll give it my best shot."

It was obvious by the next morning that their original plans for small and simple didn't stand a chance. Mitch had dug in his heels and refused to give an inch until Jordan went to work on him. She didn't try to bully him; she just quietly came at it from another angle. She was at Fairhaven doing his Goods and Services Tax submission, and she came into his office, ostensibly to talk business with him. Her arms folded, she leaned against the door frame, looking every inch a businesswoman. There was a brief lull, then she threw her hat into the ring. "I know everybody has been hammering on you all morning to change your plans," she said quietly. "And whatever you and Maria want is fine with Murphy and me. But..." She hesitated, the "but" indirectly telling him what they had planned was *not* okay.

Leaning back in his chair, Mitch folded his arms and stared at her, getting really fed up with this whole scene.

Accurately reading his hostile body language, Jordan stared back, her eyes lighting up with amusement. "Okay. So I'm sticking my nose in like everybody else. And honestly, whatever you two decide—fine. I just wanted you to consider it from a different perspective."

Mitch tried to relax the set of his jaw, but his tone was still testy. "Which is?"

Jordan looked down and picked at a slub in her suit jacket, then met his gaze again, her eyes sober. "I don't know what the whole deal is between you and Maria, and I don't want to know. But I expect that for her, marriage, whatever the circumstances are, has some fairly significant meaning. I would hate to see you minimize her values, Mitchell, that's all."

His arms still folded, he continued to stare at his sister-in-law, thinking about what she'd said. Finally he spoke. "You have a point."

She gave him a small smile. "Yes, I do."

"So what do you suggest?"

She shrugged. "Well, I was thinking of maybe a small ceremony here, just for the family and maybe the staff. It wouldn't take much work to fix up the small greenhouse—it would be a beautiful setting, Mitch. And we could have a little reception after—nothing extravagant. Just a bit of a celebration." There was a coaxing look in her big gray eyes. "She's had so many hardships, Mitch. She deserves a nice wedding, no matter what the circumstances."

Mitch experienced a twist of amusement. She was slick, this sister-in-law of his. And as smooth as silk. But she did have a point. It had never entered his head, about the wedding part, and the last thing he wanted was for Maria to feel cheated.

He continued to stare at Jordan a moment, assessing his options. Finally he spoke, a stern tone in his voice. "So if I let you run with this, I can count on you to hold it at that?"

Straightening up and standing ramrod straight, she lifted her right hand as if taking an oath, an untrustworthy glint in her eyes. "On my honor."

He watched her. "You swear?"

She held back a grin but kept her hand up. "I swear."

"And no presents. Maria would feel very uncomfortable about receiving presents."

"No presents."

Having a feeling he was going to regret this, he sighed. "Okay, Jordan. Make out whatever checks you need on my personal checking account, and I'll sign 'em. And get her something nice to wear. But," he said, leveling a finger at her, "you'd better stick to your part of the deal, or I'll have you up for professional misconduct."

Laughing at him, she gave him a thumbs-up sign and turned, and he heard her mutter to herself as she walked away, "Damn, but I'm good."

The date was set for the following Saturday, and Mitch had no idea that small and simple could create such a fuss. Going shopping for a new suit for himself and Grandfather Rodriguez, getting a marriage license, ordering extra flowers and a cake, arranging for a caterer, lining up a Justice of the Peace—it was absolutely nuts.

He hated to think what it would have been like if he'd given Jordan a whole month to plan something small and simple. It was getting so out of control, he half expected Jordan to march in, insisting they had to have a mariachi band. He had no idea that small and simple could cost so much, either, but he kept his mouth shut and just signed the checks.

Figuring the wedding was as good an excuse as any, he took the two boys to one of the upper end shopping centers. Once there, he turned them over to a young clerk in a trendy store who looked as if he knew a thing or two about young adult fashion, then set a limit and left. Hell, what did he know about the subject?

Maria had a fit when they got home, but there wasn't a darned thing she could do about it. He'd made sure all the price tags had been stripped off the purchases before they ever left the store.

Even with all the crazy commotion, it did strike him, though, that his family all acted, with the exception of Murphy, as if this whole thing were for real. The way they were carrying on, you would have thought this was the union of the century. He had to wonder about their enthusiasm. And their obliviousness. And he also wondered just how big Baba's smirk would be.

On top of everything else, he had to pick out a wedding band. Selecting a ring was something he wanted to do on his own. He didn't stop to figure out why, but it was really important to him that he get Maria something especially nice. Yeah, they could have made do with a simple gold band, but he knew she had had to make do her entire life, and probably had never had anything that was even a little extravagant. And he wanted the ring to be special. Something she could keep afterward, something that would be hers.

It took some looking, but he found what he wanted. The band was very wide, with detailed engraving and eight perfect diamonds. It was a bold ring; there was nothing soft and demure about it. With the gold and diamonds, it was her, somehow—the warmth of gold, the flash and fire of diamonds, and it would suit her long, slender hand perfectly. On the spur of the moment, he bought a second ring—a plain wide band for himself. Hell, they might as well do it up right.

He probably would have never made it through the week if it hadn't been for Maria. He was so busy keeping it together for her benefit that he didn't have time to think about himself and what he was getting into. His bride-to-be was a nervous wreck. She was all over the place—one minute appalled at the fuss, then all in a panic about what they were doing. The very next minute she would be so excited about something, she'd be practically walking on air. By Friday, she was wandering around in a daze, as if she didn't know what end was up. Jordan finally bundled her up at two in the afternoon and took her home with her. Which was part of the plan—that Maria would spend Friday night with Jordan. And Mitch picked up little whisperings that seemed to be about some sort of surprise the Munroe women had planned.

Although he wouldn't have admitted it to a living soul, by Friday night, Mitch wasn't sure he knew one end from the other, either. And he didn't stop pacing until a very special delivery arrived by courier from a Vancouver florist. A delivery of very special flowers. Edgy and anxious to have the ceremony over and done with, he probably wouldn't have slept a wink, except that Murphy took him out and got him drunk. But Mitch used his head. He stuck with tequila.

Saturday bloomed as a perfect spring morning—sun shining, not a cloud in the sky, clear and warm. It couldn't have been more perfect if Mitch had special ordered it. It was a great day, an up-and-at-'em morning. He was so calm, relaxed and laid-back, it was almost scary. And he didn't have a single doubt about what he was about to do. This was going to be a piece of cake.

The wedding was at three. Murphy, who was standing up for him, showed up at 2:10 p.m. with his two sons, all three of them decked out to the nines. Then his mother arrived about 2:30 p.m. to make sure they all passed inspection, including the Rodriguezes. She suggested they stay up there, in the apartment, out of everyone's way, and Murphy rolled his eyes behind her back. Mitch grinned and shrugged his shoulders. He might have guessed; Ma was taking over the show. After she left, Mitch gave Murphy the rings, and Murphy gave a low whistle of appreciation when he saw Maria's. He stuck them both in his breast pocket, then looked at Mitch, a wicked sparkle in his eyes. "I see you finally smashed that piggy bank, bro."

Mitch didn't even give him the satisfaction of a response. By 2:35 p.m. there were a surprising number of cars in the parking lot, considering they had stuck a large sign at the turn-off for the access road, notifying potential customers that Fairhaven Nurseries was closed for the day. But Mitch ignored the parking lot traffic and poured his father two fingers of Scotch. He was going to be deaf, dumb and blind until somebody sent for them.

It was two minutes to three when Jordan entered the apartment, looking like an angel in something purple and gauzy that came to her knees, with a purple, shimmery ribbon woven through her blond hair. She looked great, but her smile was a little strained when she met his gaze. "Could I talk to you for a minute, Mitch?"

Experiencing a feeling of apprehension in his gut, Mitch set down his glass of soda water and crossed the room. He followed his sister-in-law out into the hallway.

Closing the door behind him, he asked simply, "What's up?"

She glanced down the hallway, then gave him a helpless shrug. "We had a little bridal shower for Maria last night, and I think that kind of threw her. She got up this morning with a bad case of nerves. She's upset—and she's feeling guilty because she's misleading everyone."

Mitch let his pent-up breath go in a rush. Nerves he could take care of. "Where is she?"

"In the staff room downstairs."

Mitch started down the hallway. "Fine," he answered, his tone clipped. "Get everybody organized and ready to roll. I'll take care of it."

He didn't know why, but his heart was pounding by the time he reached the staff room. He opened the door, his insides doing barrel rolls when he saw her. Her dark hair was done up in an elaborate braid, with a wide crown of pink and white spring flowers encircling her head. She had on a gauzy pink dress that swirled around her knees when she turned to face him. And she looked so damned beautiful, it made his chest hurt just to look at her.

"Wow," he murmured, his tone awestruck.

She tried to smile, but it just wouldn't come. "I am so scared, Mitchell," she whispered.

Crossing the room, he took both of her hands in his. They were as cold as ice, and he pressed them flat against his chest, covering them securely with his own. His voice was soft and husky when he spoke. "You have nothing to be afraid of, Maria."

She gazed up at him, her expression stricken. "But it has become a wedding, Mitchell."

He understood entirely where she was coming from, and he chuckled, giving her hands a reassuring squeeze. "Nah. It's a party, honey." His expression softened and he gazed into her eyes. "And it's a celebration because you and the boys get to stay in Canada. And because you get to be a real part of the family."

She expelled her breath in a rush and turned her hands over so she could grip his. This time she managed a smile that was almost real. "We are not doing something very wrong?"

"Nope. We aren't doing one thing wrong. This is very right."

The anxious look was back in her eyes. "You are sure?"

He smiled at her. "I'm sure."

Maria swallowed hard. "I do not think I can walk in there alone, Mitchell."

Holding her gaze, he smiled again. "Fine. Then we'll walk in together."

"Is that not against the rules?"

Wanting to hug her, Mitch chuckled. "Who gives a damn? We'll make up our own rules."

She let out another big breath and squared her shoulders. "I am ready. We will do this thing."

Mitch gave her hand one last squeeze, then let go. "Hold on. You're missing something."

He went over to the fridge and took out two large bouquets, stripping the plastic wrapping off both. A medley of fragrances filled the air. Leaving one on the counter, he took the huge bouquet of gardenias, white roses and lilies of the valley to her. His expression was unsmiling as he gave it to her. "These are for you."

Completely stunned, she took the flowers and lightly touched one of the gardenias, then looked up at him, her eyes suddenly glimmering with tears. She didn't say anything for a moment, then she touched the flowers again and whispered unevenly, "Is so, so beautiful, Mitchell." She glanced at him, her eyes full. "Thank you so very much." Carefully blotting her eyes with one finger, she finally smiled. "How did you know about gardenias—that they are my favorite?"

Because you smell of them all the time, the little voice in his head responded. *And they will always remind me of you.* Wanting to touch her in the worst way, he took an uneven breath and answered, "Because you wore one in your hair."

She smelled the bouquet, then looked up at him, and he offered her his arm. "So, madam. Are you ready to get this show on the road?"

Slipping her arm through his, she hugged it against her. "I am ready." He gave her hand a squeeze, then reached over and picked up the other bouquet, the one of white calla lilies. Those were for Jordan.

It went like clockwork. There was the minor break with tradition at the beginning. Instead of Murphy and Mitch waiting at the front for Jordan to precede Maria down the borrowed, royal-purple runner, Murphy walked down the aisle with Jordan, followed by Maria and Mitch.

Even as calm as he was, Mitch was pretty much bowled over as he and his wife-to-be entered the small greenhouse. Between his family and his staff, they had turned it into a veritable indoor garden, with bowers of flowers everywhere. And amid the bouquet of fragrances, the scent of leftover Easter lilies overlaid all the others. It was spectacular.

It also took him about two seconds to figure out how come there were so many cars in the parking lot. All their regular Thursday seniors were there, along with several other regular customers, including Mrs. V.B.

When they reached the front and stopped before the Justice of the Peace, Mitch could feel Maria trembling beside him. Squeezing her hand, he looked down at her, giving her a grin and a little wink. He could feel the tension leave her body, and she gave him a real smile and winked back, then rolled her eyes. He wanted to laugh.

Just as a precaution against another bout of nerves, he held her hand through the entire ceremony. But what he would always remember, besides how lovely she looked and how perfect it was, was the totally overwhelmed expression on her face when he slipped the ring on her finger. She hadn't been expecting that. Nor had she been expecting the double-ring ceremony, and he could tell from her misty eyes that she was deeply touched.

But there was something else he hadn't been expecting, and that was the weird, light-headed feeling he got when she slipped that wide gold band on his finger. For one electrifying instant, it was as if it *was* all for real. He was expecting his mother to cry. Which she did. He expected his sisters to cry. Ditto for that. And he expected his nieces and nephews to throw confetti—which they did.

What he had not expected was for it to feel so real. And he definitely had not expected Maria's soft chaste kiss to nearly knock his socks off either. In fact, it pretty much knocked him senseless. But he put that down to faulty wiring in his brain, just like he'd done with the hot, erotic dreams. It wouldn't happen again. He'd have to compartmentalize that reaction just like he had compartmentalized everything else in his life. Hell, it was no big deal. He'd just married his tequila buddy.

It turned out to be quite a bash. Mr. Felder from Immigration did show up, responding to Jordan's invitation. And Mitch's father got him dead drunk. And a mariachi band, resplendent in big black sombreros and red velvet boleros, swept in about ten minutes after the ceremony—only they weren't on his tab. This one was on Murphy's. His brother had hired them to serenade the newlyweds, and the look of absolute amazement on Maria's face was something to behold. It turned out that Grandfather Rogriguez knew a thing or two about mariachi, and the band stayed until three in the morning. As did everyone else.

Mitch couldn't remember laughing so much. It was about midnight, when everything should have started winding down, that he coaxed Maria, who was sitting on his knee, surreptitiously flashing her ring under the table, into giving everyone tequila drinking lessons.

And that really blew the lid off everything. Then Roberto and Enrico decided to teach Cora and Jordan how to salsa, and pretty soon Mrs. V.B. and one of the band members were up doing a very steamy and dramatic tango. It was some bash, all right. The whole show might have cost a small fortune, but it was worth every penny.

It was well past four by the time Mitch got all the leftover booze put away and the candles blown out. Maria was waltzing around, picking up plastic glasses and old napkins, acting as if she could do another six hours. His tie was undone, his collar unbuttoned, and someone—he thought it was Baba—had spilled red wine down the front of his white shirt. And his brand new wife had dumped wedding cake in his lap. He was beginning to feel as if he'd crawled out of somebody's laundry basket.

Looping his arm around Maria's shoulder, he aimed them both toward the exit. "Come on, Mrs. Munroe. It's time to call it a night."

She gave a soft laugh and slid her arm around his waist, a somewhat surprised tone in her voice. "I am Mrs. Munroe."

"Yes, you are."

Grateful that the staircase was wide enough for both of them to go up side by side, they plodded up one step at a time. "We had ourselves quite a party."

"Yes, we did." She poked her thumb into his waist, and he looked at her. She grinned up at him. "And Mrs. Van Beuren," she said, pursing her lips and waggling her free hand suggestively, "now, she knows the tango. She could give lessons."

He shook his head and laughed, recalling his very

proper customer cutting loose. "She had a good time, that was for sure."

They managed to get through the fire door leading to the private quarters without separating, and they moseyed down the dimly lit corridor, the scent of gardenias still clinging to her. "Hey, you were supposed to throw your bouquet."

"Ha," she snorted. "It is safe in the refrigerator. I was not going to throw away such a beautiful bouquet."

Her response pleased him for some reason, and he gave her a little hug. "Good for you."

They reached their respective doorways, and it struck him that it was nice, having her directly across the hall. So close. So very close. Now if he could only get his arm from around her shoulder and let her go...

His face suddenly feeling as if it were made out of wood, he reached in front of her and opened her door, then swallowed hard, his whole body reluctant and rebelling. Needing just a second—just a moment more with her—he eased in a tight breath and rested his forehead against hers. "We had a good wedding, Mrs. Munroe," he whispered, his voice unusually husky.

She tightened her arm around him and he thought he heard her breath catch and falter. She pressed her head tight against his. "Yes, we did."

Forcing himself to get a grip, he straightened and reluctantly withdrew his arm, then brushed a kiss against her hair. "Good night, Maria."

He felt her grasp the back of his jacket, then without looking at him, she reached up and kissed his cheek. "Good night, Mitchell," she whispered unevenly.

Then she turned and disappeared into her apartment, closing the door softly behind her.

Hanging on for dear life, he entered his own apartment and shut the door behind him, then turned and jammed his forehead against the wall. His heart was pounding like a freight train, his lungs laboring, his legs suddenly so weak he could barely stand.

Closing his eyes in a grimace of pure agony, he tried to regulate his breathing, tried to shut down the heavy, unsatisfied throbbing in his body, tried to kill the surge of want. This wasn't supposed to happen, this damned response to the brush of her mouth against his skin. He wasn't supposed to want her, but by God, he did. And he wanted her with every breath, every heartbeat—and with a grinding need that went right through him. He blindly turned, ripped off his jacket and yanked his shirt free as he headed for the bathroom. He didn't know if a cold shower would shut down all his systems, but he was going to find out.

As wedding nights went, it was definitely a bust. He didn't sleep, and he tried to drink himself into a stupor, but that didn't work, either. Nothing worked. But a five-kilometer run finally did the trick. It did the trick, all right; it nearly killed him. Man, he had to get a grip. He couldn't let himself get off track. It was a straightforward business arrangement; it had nothing to do with fantasizing about conjugal visits. Although he wondered, as he was taking his third shower in as many hours, if maybe he shouldn't have let Maria remove the conjugal aspect of marriage during their negotiations.

Disgusted with himself, he stepped out of the shower and got ready to go to work. He needed to give his head a shake. Hell, he needed to get his head together. One way or another, he was going to have to haul his brain above his belt buckle. If he stayed focused it would not be a problem. He could do that. Okay, so he'd slipped up once, but it wasn't going to happen again. All he had to do was stay focused.

Two weeks into his legalized, sanctified marriage of agreement—his unconsummated marriage of agreement—Mitch realized he'd known nothing about problems. He'd been totally naive. But after two weeks with Maria as his wife, he now knew all about problems. The new Mrs. Munroe was giving him fits. Not only had she started managing his entire life, he could swear she was trying to drive him crazy.

Right from the beginning there was the constant elusive scent of gardenias that drifted around behind her. And always, always, beneath the fragrance, there was the warm, womanly scent of her.

And she somehow kept rearranging his life. His apartment had never been so clean and orderly, although he didn't have a clue when she managed to scour, scrub and dust. For the first time since he'd left home, his laundry disappeared from the floor and reappeared a day later, his socks perfectly matched and rolled, his underwear folded. Even the missing buttons had been replaced on his favorite shirt. She also nagged him about eating regularly, about taking care of himself. And at least three times a week, a casserole, with all the Mexican flavors and textures, would show up in his fridge. He was developing a fetish for casseroles. He knew exactly where she was every minute of the day. And nights? Hell, he didn't even dare

think about the nights. There were times he was so
aware of her, he'd swear he could hear her breathing
through the walls. And he couldn't count the nights
he had come awake, so hot and so hard he was ready
to climb the walls. Nights when he was so aroused he
was ready to claw his way through wood.

He was getting testier by the day. He knew it. He
did a lot of deep, controlled breathing, but every once
in a while, he'd come within an inch of losing it.

He knew one Monday morning—a bright, sunny
May morning—was not getting off to a good start
when he slept in. And had to drive the boys to classes
before the coffee was ready.

Jessica, who worked for the Calgary Board of Education, had arranged for an assessment for both of
them to determine their grade level. Then Mitch had
enrolled them in a private learning center, to get them
up to speed before they entered regular school in the
fall.

As soon as he dropped the boys off, he stopped at
a drive-through and got the largest, strongest cup of
coffee he could buy, but by then it was too late. He
was just plain cranky.

When he got back to Fairhaven, he was met with
the news that Abel had wrecked the forklift attachment
for the Bobcat, then a shipment of shrubs had arrived
two days early—which was a major pain to unload
without the forklift.

The whole day was like that. If it wasn't one thing,
it was another, until Mitch was ready to bite somebody's head off.

It was going on six o'clock when he found himself
out back in the annex, helping the extra part-time staff

unload a shipment of annuals that had finally arrived—only four hours later than expected. He was hot and he was hungry, and he had just about run out of patience when Doris came whipping around the corner, perky as hell. "Hey, Boss is it okay if I put the *Paeonia lactiflora* with the *Paeonia officinalis,* or do you want it put with the *Papaver orientale?*"

Mitch had it up to the teeth with her *Paeonia lactiflora* and her *Papaver orientale.* Slamming down a tray of petunias and yanking off his gloves, he turned to face her. "For God's sake, will you speak English? I haven't got a bloody clue what you're talking about."

Her head came up and she jammed her hands on her hips, giving him a snotty look. "Do you," she said, speaking very slowly and very loudly, as if he was both deaf and stupid, "want me to put the Chinese peonies with the regular peonies, or do you want me to put them with the Oriental poppies?" She gave him a smarmy smile. "You know Oriental poppies—those are the big orange ones with the big black centers."

Resisting the urge to throw something, he glared at her. "I don't care. Do what you want. You will, anyway."

She flipped her nose at him, then turned around and wiggled her butt. "Huffy, puffy. Daddy needs a new pair of shoes."

Mitch felt like his veins were all going to explode, but he ground his teeth together, yanked his gloves back on and loaded the last of the flats onto the welded steel racks.

As soon as everything was unloaded and the crew gone, Mitch stripped off his gloves for the last time and entered the greenhouse, his shirt soaked with sweat. Picking up the bottled water, he turned his face up and squeezed the container, using the cool liquid to wash away his sweat.

He was just setting the bottle down when Maria flounced in, hot Latin temper snapping in her eyes. She had on a bright blue-and-green, full skirt and a white blouse with ruffles around the neck that looked like it had come from some Mexican dance troop. Slamming her hands on her hips, she gave him a heated look. "You were rude to Doris, Mitchell."

He wiped the water off his face, then glared at her. "Stay out of it, Maria. It's none of your affair."

She came forward, her hips swinging. "It is my affair. When you are rude to my friend, it is very much my affair, Mitchell."

His own temper climbing a couple of notches, he smacked his leather work gloves down on the shelf. "Look," he growled. "I've just about had it. If it hasn't been one damned thing today, it's another. So if Doris's feelings are hurt, too bad."

But Maria had no intention of giving it up, and she came over to him and poked him in the chest. "I never said her feelings were hurt. I said you were rude. One is not *rude,* Mitchell."

"Is that your new word for the day?"

Fireworks went off in her eyes, and she got a look on her face that probably would have thrown the fear of God into anyone else. Mitch was too fed up to pay much attention. In a royal snit, she poked him several more times in the chest, her whole body sending off sparks, her breasts heaving. "You," she muttered, poking him again. "You are an animal."

He could smell her; he could smell the heat of her, the perspiration on her skin. And all of a sudden, he couldn't take it anymore. There was just too much heat, too much Latin passion, and she was just too close.

Without a single thought to self-preservation, Mitch grasped her face and shut her up the only way he knew how—with a kiss hot enough to incinerate rocks. And the instant his mouth covered hers, a storm of plain old lust nearly scorched his perfectly matched socks to ashes. Suddenly, holding her face was not enough— not nearly enough. Giving in to the driving need, he thrust one hand into her hair, locking her hot, lush mouth against his. Then he clamped his other arm around her hips, dragging her soft, lush body against his groin.

His mind and body had been primed for this for so long, it was like touching flame to tinder. And suddenly he couldn't breathe, he couldn't move; all he could do was taste and feel. The softness of her breasts, the heat of her body against his, the hot honey taste of her mouth...

There was a split second of conscious thought, when he might have been able to pull back. But then she made a low sound and slid her arms around his waist, yielding her mouth to him. And right then, Mitch lost it. His heart in a frenzy, his body screaming for more, he widened his stance and dragged her up hard against him, until her pelvis was flush with his. With his hand tangled in her thick hair, he drank from her mouth, starved for the taste of her. She twisted against him, and lights exploded behind his eyes, his whole body humming with a heavy, pulsating heat.

There could be no turning back. He'd never survive if they did.

He was enveloped in heat—his, hers—and he felt as if he were drowning in it. And he knew he was a nanosecond away from totally losing control.

Then all of sudden, ice cold water poured down on them. It was such a shock that it took Mitch a few seconds to get his wits about him, to realize the misting sprinklers had come on. Only the sprinkler they were standing under was obviously broken, and it was dumping water out like an open faucet.

Before he really figured out what had hit him, Maria was gone, and he was left standing there, the water pouring over him doing little to put out the fire inside. Closing his eyes, he bent his head and rested his hands on his hips, so damned aroused even his teeth ached. Man, he was in big trouble now. Because his erotic dreams had just become reality.

Chapter 7

Mitch never slept a wink that night. After the mind-blowing encounter in the greenhouse, Maria had simply disappeared. Later, when he'd finally been able to walk, he had gone looking for her, not sure what he was going to say, but knowing he had to say something. He hadn't been able to find her anywhere.

He heard her come home late, close to midnight, and he stood at his door for fifteen minutes, debating whether he should confront her or not. But he decided cornering her in her own apartment was a pretty lousy thing to do. And he was a big enough louse already. Besides, he didn't really trust himself yet, and he wasn't entirely sure what he would do if he got that close to her. In this instance, caution was probably a smart move—a conclusion he should have come to *before* he grabbed her in the greenhouse. He was simply going to have to put his mind to it, and get it together.

That was a joke. He was still reeling at 7:00 a.m., in such bad shape that he wasn't sure he could find the Bow River if he were standing in it.

And he sure as hell couldn't find Maria. All day, once again, everybody else had seen her except him. Finally deciding she'd figured out something he hadn't, he gave up. If she didn't want to talk to him, he wasn't going to force the issue. It didn't make any difference, one way or another. He'd just leave her alone until she was ready to come talk to him.

It was a good plan. Except after an entire week of more erotic dreams, practically no sleep and being unable to eat, Mitch couldn't take it anymore. He was going to have to do something.

He'd seen her leave right after she finished work, and he had watched her catch the city transit bus. She had gone somewhere. Knowing she was going to have to come home sooner or later, and walk down the hallway to get to her apartment, he came up with another plan. It still didn't seem right for him to corner her in her private sanctuary. But she was his wife, for God's sake; surely a man had a right to talk to his *wife*. So he was simply going to stoop to underhanded tactics, and ambush her.

He left his apartment door open a crack, and waited. And waited. It was nearly eleven o'clock that night when he heard the fire door open at the end of the hallway. Careful not to make a sound, he went to his door.

Hearing the rattle of plastic in the hallway, he made his move. Without any kind of warning, he grabbed her. Clamping his hand over her mouth, he got her in a body lock and hauled her into his apartment, kicking the door closed behind him. "You've dodged me for long enough, lady," he muttered, struggling to hang on to her squirming body. "It's time we had a talk."

She was a whole lot stronger than she looked, and she put up one hell of a fight. Pretty sure she wouldn't scream and bring the house down, he removed his hand from her mouth and locked his arm across her chest, welding her tightly against him. "Just give it up, Maria. I'm not letting you go until you promise you're going to talk to me."

Her tone seething, she let go a spate of Spanish, and he was pretty sure she wasn't telling him to have a nice day. Muttering another phrase, she twisted in his hold, and suddenly they were chest to chest, belly to belly, and the feel of her plastered against him—soft and warm and smelling so damned good—was just too much.

And there was no way he could stop himself. Spanning the back of her head with his hand, he found her mouth, a hot driving need coursing through him, and in that instant, his resolve crashed like a ton of bricks. He was in such sensory overload, he was drowning in the taste of her, in the feel of her, and it wasn't enough. Not nearly enough. He wanted it all.

It was the taste of blood that snapped him out of it—his, hers; he couldn't tell. But knowing he might have hurt her stopped him dead in his tracks. It wasn't until he backed off that he realized he'd crushed her handbag and small parcel between them.

His face contorting from the sheer agony of having to let her go, he closed his eyes and slammed himself back against the closet, his heart thundering against his chest wall, his blood running thick and heavy. God, he had lost it again. All he'd wanted to do was talk to her, and he had gone at her like some sort of wild rutting animal. How in hell would he ever be able to explain this away?

He expected to hear the door slam from her leaving. Instead, he experienced a fluttering touch against his face, then the warmth of her palm against his cheek. It took nearly all the strength he had to open his eyes and look at her.

Her mouth swollen and still wet from his, she gazed up at him, a gentleness in her eyes he'd never seen before. Giving him an uneven smile, she pressed the small package into his hand. "I brought you a present," she whispered unevenly. "And I want to change part of our bargain. If you agree."

Mitch stared at her, his pulse going berserk again, knowing from the size and shape exactly what was in the package. He got slammed with such a hot and heavy rush, he thought his lower body just might explode. And he simply could not breathe.

She gave him another unsteady smile, and for an instant, he thought his knees were going to buckle beneath him. Then she touched him again, and a crazy kind of relief poured through him. So overcharged he could barely think, he stripped the strap of her handbag off her shoulder and dropped it on the floor. Then, clenching his teeth against another hot rush, he swept her up and started down the hallway, his heart thundering as he crushed her against him. Slipping her arms around him, she buried her face against his neck and hung on, as if he were rescuing her.

Once in his bedroom, he dropped the package on his night table and set her down, his face rigid with restraint. What he wanted to do was dump her on the bed and pull her under him, but he knew the instant he felt her beneath him there would be no way he'd be able to stop. And when that finally happened, he wanted not a single item of clothing between them. She had on the frilly white blouse and the full green-and-blue skirt. Bracing himself, he clenched his jaw and reached out, yanking the blouse up over her head. His heart nearly stopped altogether when he discovered she was naked underneath. Battling for control, his whole body clenched, he was about to undo the zipper of his jeans when he felt her hands on his waistband. The jolt of anticipation he got was so strong, so debilitating, he had to close his eyes and rest his forehead against hers, a violent shudder coursing through him.

After she shoved his jeans away, it was almost more than he could manage to undo the button at her waist and slide his hands down her hips, stripping away the rest of her clothes.

Fighting for control, he lifted her up and carried her to the bed, coming down on top of her. Experiencing for the first time her totally naked beneath him, he shut his eyes, a hoarse sound wrenched from him by the rush of hot, hot pleasure. This was no dream. It was real. Unable to stop himself, he rocked his hard ridge of flesh against her.

She made a soft desperate sound, and somehow that sound freed him from his own driving need. And suddenly, it wasn't about him anymore. It was all about her.

He was a skilled lover, and a thorough one. But first, before he got so lost in her he couldn't trust himself, he took care of the protection. Then he gave in to the awful need to touch her, to touch and taste all of her. Every inch. Every curve. Every hollow. One by one, he stroked and tasted every sensate point, every pulsating part of her body, using his hands and mouth to stimulate her, to arouse her, to bring her to the very edge. Because without giving her all the gratification there was to experience, it would be empty and meaningless. This was not just an act of sex. Not with Maria.

So focused on her that he was able to ignore the hot, throbbing clamor in his own body, he saturated himself with the taste and warmth of her. Then he finally returned to suckle her breast, drawing her deeper and deeper inside his mouth as he stroked the juncture of her thighs. She cried out and arched up against the pressure of his hand, and he moved on top of her, his control shattering. He needed to be inside her. He needed her.

Entering her slowly, he clutched her beneath him, desperation claiming him, the pleasure so intense it nearly took him under. Unable to stop himself, he started to move, the urgent thrusting rhythm echoing in his brain. His mind in a red-hot fog, he felt her peak and arch beneath him, rising up to meet the final ecstasy. Covering her mouth to stifle her cries, he groaned and let himself go, his release coming with such force that it paralyzed him. And all that he was aware of was that he was safe in the warm, wet cradle of her body, wrapped in the very essence of her. In a place he had never been in before.

In the past, with every other woman he had been with, the experience of climaxing had always been a solitary sensation—him alone in the dark place of his sensory center, awash in that paralyzing feeling of release. But this time—this time it was different. This time it was like falling into an ocean of sensations, each one stronger, more powerful than the last. This time it was like nothing he had ever experienced before—because she was in that same dark, sensory place with him, locked in a dance of raw, hot desire. And he was so aware of her, it was as if she was right inside him. This was more—far more than he'd ever imagined. And far more than he had ever bargained for.

It took him a long, long time to recover, and an even longer time to regain enough strength to stir. The only reason he forced himself to move was that he knew he was far too heavy for her.

Marshaling every ounce of strength he had, he dragged himself up and braced his weight on his elbows. Then, bracketing her face with his hands, he bent his head and covered her mouth in a soft, gentling kiss, trying to tell her without words how special it had been. He felt stripped naked inside, so raw he couldn't talk. He was too exposed to talk. All he wanted was to stay where he was for the rest of his natural life.

The dampness of tears collected against his thumbs and he shifted her head, this time to kiss her eyes. He was pretty sure she had experienced a climax, but he had been so far gone by that point, he couldn't be absolutely positive. Finished with her eyes, he tipped her head back and kissed her mouth again. "Are you okay?" he asked softly, his voice very husky.

She nodded and took an unsteady breath. "I am..." she whispered unevenly, pausing to search for the appropriate word, "...very splendid." She ran her hand across his bare back. "And you?"

Feeling as spent and as stripped naked as he did, Mitch was surprised to find himself grinning. "I'm very splendid, too," he answered, then kissed her mouth again.

She gave his hair a little tug and he lifted his head. "Are you making fun of my English, Mitchell?"

A kind of satiated contentment oozed through him, and he no longer felt quite so raw and exposed. Finally regaining some control, finally able to meet her gaze without being afraid she might find something in his eyes, he lifted his head and looked down at her. The light from the hallway provided enough illumination for him to see her face. "Yes," he said, trying not to grin. "I am."

She narrowed her eyes and pinched his back, and he chuckled and kissed her again. And suddenly, out of nowhere, this overwhelming feeling came over him. This urge to ask how it really was for her, to tell her that she had been terrific and had given him something he'd never experienced before. He wanted to tell her about the dreams he'd been having about her, and how she'd been driving him crazy for weeks. And maybe she would tell him what it had been like for her, and why she had gone out and bought the condoms. But he had always been bad at that part, the talking-afterward part. And besides his rotten record, there was something else he had to be careful of—of getting too close, too intimate. He knew better.

But he wasn't prepared to let her go, either. Closing his eyes, he slid his arms back around her and tightened his hold, breathing in the scent of her. He knew he couldn't stay inside her for very much longer; it was something he just couldn't risk. He was so sensitized though, it was going to be like stripping flesh. He gave himself another second. Then, bracing himself, he gritted his teeth and abruptly withdrew. He gave himself a second to recover. Then holding her securely against him, he rolled onto his back, taking her with him. Having her draped all over him felt good, and he swept her hair back and kissed her throat; then he nestled her head against the curve of his neck, aware of every warm, soft inch of her. Slowly combing his fingers through the thick masses of her hair, he reveled in how great it felt to be able to hold her like that.

She caressed the shape of his ear. "This is very nice, Mitchell," she whispered, her voice a little uneven. He lifted his head and kissed her shoulder, then gave her a squeeze. "It's better than nice."

There was a little pause, then she spoke again. "Have you been waiting a long time?"

He wasn't sure if she was asking if he'd been waiting a long time for her to get home, or if he'd been waiting a long time to get her into bed. He figured after he'd spent the last hour ravishing her, she deserved an honest answer. He responded with a low chuckle. "A very, very long time."

He felt her smile against his neck. "I think you liked the present I brought for you."

That made him really laugh, and he gave her a hard hug. "I loved the present you brought me."

She shivered, and he reached down, just managing to snag the tumbled sheet on his unmade bed. He pulled it up and tucked it under her chin, then wrapped his arms around her, knowing he had to give some sort of explanation before she put her own spin on it.

Trying to think of what to say and how to say it, he continued to comb his fingers through her silky hair. Finally he drew a deep breath. "I didn't plan for this to happen, Maria," he said quietly.

He felt her go very still, and he knew that he had put it badly and she had misunderstood. Tightening his hold on her so she couldn't get away, he nuzzled his nose against her fragrant skin. "I didn't want you avoiding me any longer because of what happened in the greenhouse." He smoothed down her hair, then cupped the back of her head, drawing her closer. "The truth is, I was pretty much in a tailspin after that," he said, his voice even more gruff. "I convinced myself if I dragged you in here, I'd have a chance to say what I had to say." He ran his hand through her hair again, then pulled it back, urging her to look at him. Meeting her gaze, he gave a lopsided smile. "But I gotta tell you. I was so glad you brought that present, honey. I was pretty far gone."

Her expression lightened, and she braced one arm on his chest, then slowly traced his bottom lip. "So you just wanted to talk."

"Yeah." He grinned at her, trapping her marauding hand. "But I liked this a whole lot better."

She laughed and leaned down, giving him the

softest kiss. "You use this kind of language very well."

There was something in her tone that made him uneasy, as if she was trying to make light of it, and he experienced a disquieted feeling. Swallowing against the sudden thick feeling in his chest, he spread his fingers across the back of her head, holding her mouth against his. "Stay," he whispered gruffly.

Her touch making his heart pound, she softly, so very gently laid her hands along his jaw, her mouth moist and tormenting. "I will stay," she breathed, then tightened her hold. But he knew by the way she said it that there was something more she didn't say. And the feeling of disquiet gave another twist.

Not liking the sensation, he opened his mouth and feasted from hers, wanting to lose himself in her. She shifted against him and kissed him back, her response taking his breath away. And once again he was swept into a thick, sensual vortex, aware of nothing but her.

Mitch had no idea how many times they made love during the night. He couldn't get enough of her, and every time, he wanted her more than before. The last time she nearly finished him off.

Afterward, it was as if the need in him had finally been slaked, and he was content to nestle her in the curve of his body and close his eyes, his body satiated, replete. And as he let sleep take him under, he knew there would be no dreams tonight. Because his dream was right there beside him.

He awoke at dawn, and he was not happy when he discovered he was alone. She might be gone, but the scent and evidence of their lovemaking was everywhere. And to make it worse, the bed was in a shambles and his body reminded him in living detail how it got that way. He lay there for twenty minutes, face-down on the tumble of bedding, trying to will away his response, wanting her all over again.

Knowing he was fighting a losing battle, he got up without another glance at the bed. Then he started sec-ond-guessing why she had left. Suddenly uptight and anxious, he had a shower and tried to get some break-fast down. But he kept listening for the sound of her door opening, and that only made it worse. Unable to stand it any longer, he went downstairs to the garden center and resorted to pacing up and down the center aisle, feeling as if he had a pack of dogs on his heels. Where was she? Wherever she was, she was probably having second thoughts about getting tied up with him.

He was an inch away from coming unglued when he heard her on the stairs, and he closed his eyes, trying to pull it together. But this kind of anxiety was totally foreign to him, and he didn't know what to do with it. It just wouldn't fit into one of his little mental compartments.

The door from the stairs opened, and Mitch felt as if his heart might climb right out of his chest when she looked up and saw him standing there. She stared at him, something dark and unreadable in her eyes. Then it was gone, and as if understanding he needed a certain reaction from her, she gave him a wry smile, flashing her dimples. Then she lifted her hands in an expressive shrug, an I-guess-we-blew-that glint in her eyes. Lord, she looked so damned beautiful, her hair loose around her face, the cornflower blue of her T-shirt doing unbelievable things to her skin, the snug-ness of her blue jeans doing unbelievable things to her lush body. Suddenly he needed to touch her like he needed to get air into his lungs. He didn't know what to say to her—what could he say? So he just acted on pure instinct. Feeling as if he were about to drown, he covered the distance between them, his heart slamming against his ribs. Hooking his arm around her neck, he pulled her to him, a crazy kind of giddiness pumping through him the minute he had her in his arms.

Closing his eyes, he tucked her head under his chin and wrapped her in a tight embrace, another ruckus starting up in his chest. Feeling as if he were twenty leagues over his head and sinking even deeper, he tightened his hold and buried his face in her hair. He felt her take a deep uneven breath; then she slipped her arms around his waist and stepped closer into his embrace, flattening her hands against his back. The panic abruptly subsided, and he gave himself ten seconds to get everything under control.

Smoothing down her hair, he pressed his mouth against her temple. "What took you so long?"

She turned her face against his neck and he felt her smile. "I did not know you were waiting, Mitchell." She ran her thumb along his spine. "Are we going someplace?"

His eyes closed, Mitch let his breath go in a huff of laughter and pressed his head tighter against hers, a familiar thickness accumulating in the lower half of his body. He knew he didn't dare hold her like that for too much longer, but he didn't want to let her go completely, either. So he hatched a plan. "How about we blow this joint and go out for breakfast?"

He felt her grasp the back of his shirt, as if needing

something more to hang on to. "But what about your store?"

Knowing he was sinking fast, he rubbed his hand up her back, his voice gruff when he answered. "Doris and Karen can manage."

Pressing her face tighter against his neck, she swallowed. "Breakfast would be nice."

He wanted to kiss her so badly he could feel it right down to the soles of his feet. But he knew if he gave in to the urge, he'd have her back upstairs and in his bed so quickly she wouldn't know what hit her. He allowed himself several more seconds, then reluctantly loosened his hold and kissed her forehead. "Come on, Mrs. Munroe. Let's go eat."

Outside she let out an exclamation, then danced backward in front of him, the wind catching her hair, delight making her eyes sparkle. "Oh, Mitchell. It is a most beautiful day!"

Behind the safety of his sunglasses, he couldn't take his eyes off her. "Beautiful," he agreed, his tone gruff. "Most beautiful."

Somehow it was easier once they were sitting across the table from each other in a back booth of Joe's Highway Diner. The place was jammed with truckers, and the smell of ham and eggs hung in the air, the clang of an old-fashioned cash register punctuating the steady noise. It was as if that back booth was an island, and the clatter and chatter flowed right around them.

It was still before seven o'clock, with the long shadows of early morning slanting across the street, where robins harvested earthworms on the meager boulevard.

They were served coffee, and placed their orders with the gum-chewing waitress, whose uniform came right out of the fifties. As soon as she was gone, Mitch looked down and slowly stirred his coffee, trying to find words to make everything right. He didn't have a clue how much sense he'd made last night. But one thing for sure, he didn't want any misunderstandings between them—and he didn't want Maria to think he was just using her. He liked her far too much.

Resting his arms on the table, he laced his hands around his mug and looked at her. She was sitting with her chin propped in her hand, watching clouds still tinged with orange and mauve. Before he had a chance to say anything, she spoke, a dreamy quality to her voice. "Your sky is most awesome, Mitchell. So big and wide. It gives the feeling of such space, of such freedom to breathe."

He studied her, experiencing an odd, unexpected connection with her. The Alberta sky had always made him feel much the same way, as if he were in a space where he could take a very deep breath. When he was away, it was the sky he missed most, then the mountains. His voice was quiet when he answered, "I know exactly what you mean."

Her chin still on her hand, she looked at him, and there was something in that look, some affinity, that made it very easy for him to say what was on his mind. His gaze fixed on her, he confessed, "I'm sorry I manhandled you last night, but I don't regret what happened, Maria. I've been wanting to take you to bed ever since that time in the greenhouse."

As olive as her skin was, she turned absolutely pink, and she gave a strangled laugh and covered her face with her hands. He hadn't meant to embarrass her, but he wasn't sorry he had. She was so adorable that he

wanted to hug her all over again. Grinning at her reaction, he just had to stick it to her a little more. "And
as for your present, I gotta tell you, it was probably
my all-time favorite and I—"

Rising up, she reached across the table and clamped
her hand over his mouth, her cheeks still pink. There
was a look of admonishment in her eyes, but there
was also a sparkle of humor. "I think I have heard
enough about my present, Mitchell," she said, her
voice catching on restrained laughter. "And I am glad
you liked it."

As if he made her just a little bit nervous, she swallowed hard and wet her bottom lip, and Mitch's heart
started to hammer. Recollections of them together in
his king-size bed made his whole body hum, totally
scrambling his thought processes. Right back in the
same aroused condition he had been earlier, he wanted
to plunk his forehead down on the tabletop, his ability
to be even halfway articulate going up in smoke. Maria was staring at him, the pulse in her neck going like
crazy, and it was as if they were wired on the exact
same wavelength.

His heart laboring under a thick, heavy weight, he
reached across the table and clasped her hand, so light-
headed he was almost dizzy. God, he had to level with
her. Somehow, he had to get the words out. Swallowing hard, he spoke, his tone low and very strained. "I
just want you to know that it felt pretty good to share
that kind of intimacy with you, Maria. And I'm glad
it happened."

Her expression unreadable, she stared at him, her
eyes so big and round he felt as if he were lost in
them. Then she turned her hand over, and the electric

sensation of being palm-to-palm with her made his heart falter. She managed a small smile, but her voice was very unsteady when she responded. "I am glad it happened, too," she said, the pulse in her throat still hammering away. "And I do not see why this kind of—sharing cannot be part of our arrangement."

Mitch wanted to close his eyes and rest his forehead on their clasped hands, a crazy relief making his whole body weak, relieved she had done such a hell of a job figuring out what he was trying to say. But there was another part of him—a tiny part—that was just a little bit annoyed that she'd made reference to the arrangement angle.

Realizing that she was watching him with big serious eyes, he set aside that sliver of annoyance and simply studied her. A twist of humor surfaced. He deliberately rubbed his palm against hers, which sent a sexual current through his entire body. He wanted to haul her across the table, but he was saved by a flicker of amusement when he saw her breath catch and her pupils constrict. Nope. He wasn't the only one who had some faulty wiring. "So," he said, his smile turning into a grin, "does this mean I get to use the rest of my present?"

She gave a little burst of laughter, her eyes widening, a flush creeping up her face. Restraining a smile, she shook her head as if scolding him; then she grinned back, showing her dimples. "Ah, Mitchell," she said, giving him a knowing look. "I think maybe you never received such a present before. No wonder you are always in such a bad temper."

He might have given in to the urge to drag her across the table and kiss her senseless for that bit of sass. But right then, the gum-chewing waitress appeared with their breakfast and slapped both plates down on the table, and he had to let go of Maria's hand. But he did level a finger at her, letting her know the game wasn't over. She laughed and flipped open her paper napkin, as if to brush off his warning. And as innocent as hell, she smiled up at the waitress, really laying on a Spanish accent. "This is excellent. My employer is very difficult to please, and he had me working overtime late into the night. And I am ravished."

"Yeah," said the waitress, snapping her gum and refilling their coffee mugs at the same time. "I know what you mean."

Nearly strangling on the need to laugh, Mitch bit the inside of his cheek to keep a straight face, then gave her a level look. "The word is *ravenous,* Maria. Not *ravished.*"

She angled her head and raised her eyebrows, giving him that imperial look. "You think so?"

Bracing his elbows on the table, he clasped his hands in front of his mouth, watching her, still struggling to keep it together. She flipped her napkin again and dropped it across her lap, pretending to ignore him as she thanked the waitress. But he saw the glint of one-upmanship in her eyes. He smothered a grin. So. Little Maria wanted to cross swords in word games did she? One thing for sure—she was a far more skilled player than he'd ever assumed her to be.

The parking lot was jammed by the time they got back to the garden center, and every available space strewn with carts. As soon as they pulled into the staff parking area, Maria was out of the truck, off to help a little old couple with their cart full of geraniums. Mitch stared after her, experiencing a shot of frustration. She was gone, and he was left standing there, feeling abandoned. He had wanted to hug her in the worst way.

He never saw her again for the rest of the morning, and he was so busy in the tree and shrubbery lot, he didn't even stop for lunch. It was spring, the threat of a late frost was nearly behind them and trays of annuals were going through the checkouts at such a speed that they had every till manned with at least two people.

It was going on six in the evening when he finally got a chance to go upstairs to grab something to eat. And he was so hot and sweaty, he decided he'd have a quick shower first. Stripping off his filthy shirt, he headed toward his bedroom and the en suite bath, but when he got to the door, he stopped short.

The bed was made, and he could see by the way the comforter was crisply folded back that the sheets and pillow cases had been changed. The image of Maria stripping that bed—that mauled and sweat-dampened bed with all the evidence of their repeated lovemaking—set off such a hell of a storm in him, he nearly buckled at the knees.

Overcome with the recollections of how it felt to be buried deep inside her, of how he could still smell the scent of them that morning, Mitch closed his eyes and rested his forehead against the door frame, his pulse suddenly racing so hard and heavy, he could hear it in his head. He needed her, just the weight of her against him to stand between him and this raw, desperate wanting.

"Mitchell, are you…" There was a whisper of movement behind him, then the touch of her hand on his naked shoulder. "Mitchell?" she whispered, her voice full of concern. "What is wrong?"

It took every ounce of willpower he had not to grab her. Fighting to quell the pounding of his blood, he raised his head and looked at her, his whole body throbbing, his mind in a fever. He tried to smile. "You made the bed."

As though he wasn't making an iota of sense, she looked from him to the bed, then back at him, a look of confusion in her eyes. Then her expression changed, and she said something in Spanish and stepped into his arms. Burying his face in her hair, Mitch locked his arms around her and hung on for dear life. Just holding her provided some relief. And he didn't even want to think about what it was going to feel like when he let her go.

Her hand on his jaw, she pressed his face around, her mouth soft and so gentle as she covered his with her own. His lungs seized up and he made a ragged sound, giving himself up to the taste of her, knowing he could lose himself forever in that kiss.

His breathing labored, he dragged his mouth away and clutched her head against him, closing his eyes and fighting for control. Pressing his face against her hair, he forced himself to take several deep breaths. "I need a shower, honey," he whispered, his voice not even sounding like his own.

She fumbled with the snap on his jeans. "You do

not need a shower, Mitchell," she murmured, undoing the zipper on his fly. "You need a siesta."

He wanted to laugh, but her knuckles brushed against his engorged flesh, and he nearly went down right there. Fighting to keep a lid on the desire clawing through him, he tried to still her hand. "Let me have a shower first."

Ignoring him, she whipped off her T-shirt, then slid her hands down his hips, dragging his jeans down. "You can have a shower later," she whispered, finding his mouth again. "First you need a rest."

A tremor coursed through him, and he grasped her face and claimed her lips, a red mist clouding his mind. He just couldn't hang on any longer. Only Maria could stop what was breaking loose inside. Only her. She was his haven in the storm.

As the following days flowed one into another, Mitch began to realize just how misguided he'd been. In the beginning, he had tried to convince himself that the sexual urgency would wear off after a few days; then he would be able to finally get a grip.

But the truth was, he spent more time in bed during that time than he had in his entire life. Nearly every night she came to him, and every night with her was the same. That desperate need to fill his senses with her. The desperate need to get inside her. The desperate need to have her there in the morning.

But that never happened. Because every morning, she was gone. And it got so he hated waking up, knowing that all that would be left was her scent. But they had got in the habit of going out for breakfast together, and that always set him back on track.

Of course, it wasn't all hugs and kisses. At times the woman drove him nuts. He never knew what would get her dander up, and lots of times she just plain refused to listen. She developed a fascination with the Bobcat, and she hounded him about teaching her how to operate it. He explained, very patiently and in great detail, that it was the busiest time of the year, and he didn't have time right then.

She tried to argue with him, reminding him in vivid detail about how he had taken the boys out driving on several occasions. He told her that the Bobcat was different from his Jeep, but she sniffed and stuck her nose in the air, telling him in no uncertain terms what she thought.

When she tackled him again Friday morning, he wasn't in the mood to try and reason with her. Nor did he have the time to get his point across, so he simply forbade her to go anywhere near the Bobcat. She flounced off as if he had offended her and trod on her independence. But that was too bad. He just bloody well didn't have time to humor her.

Later that day, just before closing time, he was outside tagging several trees for delivery to the new housing development where Murphy had constructed several homes. Mitch heard the roar of the Bobcat, and his heart jammed into his throat. Maria was behind the controls, the bucket up midway, and she was heading across the nearly empty parking lot toward the brand-new truck that he had just got for his landscaping business. It was so new it hadn't even had a chance to get dirty yet.

Her hair was flying in the breeze and there was a look of imperial smugness on her face, as if she were leading a royal parade. Seeing him standing there, his mouth hanging open, she turned and waved, her chin up in an I-guess-I-showed-you attitude. It took only a single glance for him to figure out the angle of her trajectory and expected point of impact, and he yelled at her and started running. Lifting her nose even higher, she gave him another imperial wave, then drove smack-dab into the door of his shiny new truck.

A sick feeling rose up in him when he saw how her head snapped back on the impact, and his heart was pounding out of sheer terror when he reached her. The first thing he did was immobilize her head, certain she had broken her neck.

A look of absolute horror on her face, she stared up at him, then totally misinterpreted his hands around her neck and head. "Oh, Mitchell. Are you strangling me? I am so sorry I broke your nice new truck."

Damn it, he did feel like strangling her. But not because of the bloody truck. Because she could have killed herself.

Her eyes filled with tears, and she tried to turn her head to check the damage she had done. When he held her fast, she lifted her arms and covered her face with her hands. "I am such a fool."

Figuring if she could flap her arms around that way, there was no real damage done, he took a deep, stabilizing breath and eased his hands away, a weak feeling pumping through him. "I don't care about the damned truck," he snapped. "I thought you'd broken your neck. Do you hurt anywhere?"

She dropped her hands and looked up at him, remorse making her look very young. "My neck is fine," she said in a choked voice, "but my heart is broken. Look what I did to your truck."

Man, he didn't want to do it. He did not want to smile. She had willfully disobeyed him, and now he was stuck with the consequences. But he couldn't quite contain his amusement. "I should wring your neck. I said I would teach you when I had time, Maria. But you didn't listen."

She looked so pathetic as she gazed up at him, her eyes swimming in remorse. "I did not listen. And I am so sorry, Mitchell."

Jammed in an awkward, semicrouch in the cab of the Bobcat, Mitch let go of her and rested his arms on his raised knee, studying her. He didn't even glance at his truck—his pride and joy. He didn't dare to because she looked so wretched, and so contrite. Letting his breath go in a long sigh, he tapped her hip. "Move over," he commanded. She gave him a bewildered look and did as he asked.

Climbing in beside her, he pushed himself as far back in the seat as he could get and pulled her between his thighs so she was facing forward. Reaching out on either side of her, he put his arms around her and grasped the controls. "Okay. Pay attention. This is how you put it in reverse."

He didn't deal with the wreck until next morning. Not wanting to get within ten feet of the damage she had done to his truck—and to the very pricey customized paint job he'd had done on the door—he had Abel and Karen shuttle the vehicle back to the dealership. The estimate came in just before noon. He had no idea a new door could cost that much. Still feeling shell-shocked, he dropped the quote on Jordan's desk. "When you get time, deal with this."

Her eyes grew wide and she whistled. "Wow." Then she looked up at him, clearly trying not to laugh. "Aren't you going to put this through insurance?"

He shook his head and issued a weary sigh. "No. I'm going to save our accumulated six years of accident-free coverage for the next time, when she takes a vehicle out on Highway 2 and causes a nine-car pileup."

Jordan couldn't contain herself any longer and she started to laugh. "She's very upset, you know."

He sighed again. "I know." He turned away and started for the door, then paused and glanced back at Jordan. "Don't let her know we didn't put it through insurance, okay?"

His sister-in-law flipped him a salute. "Gotcha."

As if suspecting his reason for going to the upstairs offices, Maria was waiting for him when he came back down. She was standing by the end display, wringing her hands, a stricken look on her face. "You heard from the truck place?"

Resting his hands on his hips, he considered her. "Yeah."

"You must tell me how much, so I can repay you."

It was a strange sensation, realizing that he didn't like her like this, humbled and uncertain. He liked her better when she was all fired up and angry—when she had the dignity to lift her head and stare him down. Releasing another sigh, he took her by the shoulders, then slid his hands up her neck. Hooking his thumbs under her jaw, he made her look at him. As he recalled the smug expression on her face just before impact, a little twinge of humor surfaced. He gave her a small smile. "I guess you showed me, huh?"

Horror darkened her eyes as she grasped his wrists, and for an instant he thought she might actually cry. He gave her head a gentle shake. "Hey, it was as much my fault as yours. I should have explained why I didn't want you on that thing, and I didn't. So don't sweat it."

Her eyes filled with misery, she gazed up at him. "But I disobeyed you."

He massaged her neck with the heels of his hands. "Yes you did." Amusement got the best of him, and he finally grinned. "And knowing you, you will disobey me again. I know that, and you know that."

She had the decency not to try to argue that point. Giving a little shrug, she tightened her grasp on his wrist. "But I must fix your truck, Mitchell. I was very foolish."

Not sure he could look her square in the eye and lie, he pulled her against him and wrapped his arms around her, pressing her head against him in a snug embrace. "We have insurance for that, Maria." He gave the back of her neck a little squeeze. "But I'll make a deal with you. Next time I will explain more carefully, and next time, you listen."

She finally relaxed and slid her arms around him. "I listen, Mitchell. But sometimes not with both ears."

Tightening his hold, Mitch absently rubbed his cheek against her hair. That might be so. But then there were other times she heard exactly what he wanted, without him uttering a single word.

Chapter 8

May disappeared into June, and Mitch was so busy, there were times he didn't know what day it was. He had been contracted to do a couple of pretty major landscaping jobs, and with the weather holding at near perfect, he was going flat out from dawn to dusk. Besides the major contracts, there was the ongoing contract with Munroe Construction to provide trees and shrubs in the new developments. He was in such an overload, there were a couple of times when he'd gotten out of the shower that he had to stop and think whether he was getting up or going to bed.

And the only times that he felt grounded were those nights Maria was in his bed—those unbelievable nights when she was there, like fire and silk in his arms. Those nights were what kept him going.

Then there were those other nights, when he'd get home far later than he wanted, and all the lights would be out in her apartment, and he would experience such frustration he'd want to put his fist through something.

After all those times that she had come to his bed, the situation with her should have eased off a bit, but it had only gotten worse. He spent more time thinking about her than he did about anything else. And on top of that, he found himself doing the damnedest things at the damnedest times—like stopping on his way back to town late one night, after giving a potential client an estimate, to pick her a bouquet of wild roses by the high beams on his newly restored truck.

Sometimes he almost had himself convinced that he had a grip on things, but most of the time, he felt as if he'd just been flung out of a tornado. He kept telling himself that he was bound to feel kind of tossed around, considering this was just a temporary arrangement. Except it didn't feel temporary, and it sure as hell didn't feel like any arrangement. But he filed those wayward thoughts away in some dark recess of his mind, and he just kept going forward.

He finally got a much needed break when it started raining, effectively shutting down all outdoor work. It also slowed things down at the garden center so they at least had time to catch their breath.

The rain came during the same week that his father had planned to take his grandkids into the mountains to go fishing. But a little rain wasn't going to stop Patrick Munroe. Mitch's father made the trip at least twice a year, and his grandkids loved it. The only rule was that they had to be big enough to wipe their own bums—or if they couldn't manage that on their own, they had to have a dad or an older sibling along. No moms allowed.

Papa Munroe had also extended an invitation to the most recent additions to his rat pack. The way Enrico and Roberto carried on, anyone would have thought that Papa Munroe had offered to send them on a trip into outer space.

They nearly drove their mother crazy with questions, and they were packed and ready to go at least four days in advance. Amused by Maria's exasperation, Mitch stepped in and fielded their questions. He also took the boys out and got them outfitted with lures and tackle, then dug his tent and sleeping bags out of the storage room. He had to buy more camping equipment when his father insisted that Grandfather Rodriguez had to go as well. When Mitch had them lug the works into the staff room so he could make sure they had everything they needed, Grandfather Rodriguez, a bright sparkle in his eye, waved a roll of toilet paper at Mitch. Totally appalled, Maria threw up her hands and left the room. Mitch thought Grandfather was pretty darned funny.

Murphy and Marco were going, as well as the other two sons-in-law, and as far as Mitch was concerned, that let him off the hook. He'd been on these little adventures before, and if he had a choice, he'd rather not ever go on another one if he could get out of it. It was like camping with a pack of badly behaved monkeys—and his father was the worst one of all. But the kids loved it, Papa's adventure, and so far they hadn't set each other on fire or shoved anyone down a gorge. Which said something, he guessed. And even the little ones were up to speed on ghost stories and types of trout.

Of course, he couldn't exactly overlook the fact that

with the male Rodriguezes gone, Maria would be home by herself. But by midmorning Friday, Mitch knew that any ideas of intimate dinners or all-night orgies were out the window. He'd grown up in a houseful of women and knew the signs, and he also recognized the listless eyes and the look of misery. Besides, he had spent enough time in close proximity to her, noting those nights he spent alone, that he had her dates figured out as well. With the weather pretty much shutting him down, he had been looking forward to the weekend. But it wasn't the end of the world.

The crew of campers left about three in the afternoon, and shortly after they left, Maria disappeared. It was just after five when he came across her in a corner of the staff room, her knees drawn up, her head buried in her folded arms. He could tell by the way she was rocking back and forth that she was pretty miserable. His hand on the doorknob, he considered her a minute, then spoke. "Maria?"

She lifted her head and looked at him, her eyes glassy with discomfort.

His tone was quiet. "Go upstairs and go to bed. It's not that busy."

She gave him a wan little smile, but she didn't move. He watched her for a minute, then closed the door and left. Picking up the truck keys from the information desk, he called out to Doris that he was leaving. One thing he was not dumb about was female functions. He'd heard enough about them all when he was growing up. None of his sisters were exactly shy, modest types, and they certainly didn't make a secret out of that kind of girl stuff.

When he returned from the trip to the drugstore,

Maria was no longer in the staff room. He headed up to the apartments, taking the stairs two at a time.

Not wanting to knock and wake her up if she were asleep, he cracked open the door to her apartment and listened. There wasn't a sound, and he stood there for a minute, a should-he, shouldn't-he debate going on in his head. Finally making up his mind, he quietly entered. If she was asleep, he'd leave.

He found her curled up on the sofa in the living room, her hands tucked under her face. He knew from comments that the boys had one bedroom and her father-in-law the other, which meant she had to sleep on the sofa. And although he had never said anything, that bothered the hell out of him—that she didn't even have a bed of her own.

As Mitch stood there in her surroundings, a strange sensation unfolded in his belly. With the exception of dropping off the odd bag of groceries, he hadn't so much as crossed her doorway. In fact, he had made a point of staying out of her space. He didn't want her to think that because he was basically her landlord, he had the right to intrude. But now as he stood in her living room, he felt almost displaced, as if he had just invaded some very private, unfamiliar territory.

The furniture was all the same, the drapes were the same, the color of the walls hadn't changed since he had first shown the place to her, but somehow she had changed it. Plants crowded the corners, and with various knickknacks borrowed from downstairs, and some vivid textiles she had obviously brought with her, she had put her own distinctive stamp on the apartment. She had turned it into a home, and it radiated her warmth, her sense of color, her boldness. For some reason, it made him uneasy.

Leaving the front entryway, Mitch quietly crossed the room; then he crouched down beside her and very gently tucked her hair back.

She opened her eyes and looked at him, her eyes dull, her expression waxen. Letting his hand rest on her head, he stroked her temple with his thumb. "Feeling pretty crappy?" he asked softly.

She gave a single nod and Mitch rose, then leaned down and lifted her up in his arms. The least he could do was put her to bed—in a proper bed. She started to protest, but he shushed her and gathered her closer. As if too miserable to fight, she wound her arms around his neck, then buried her face and curled up in a tight little ball.

Taking infinite care with her, he carried her from her apartment into his, and kept going until he reached his bedroom. He snagged the comforter and pulled it back, then laid her down. Bending over her, he brushed the hair off her forehead, then straightened. She didn't even open her eyes. Taking the package out of his jacket pocket, he went to the bathroom and got a glass of water. When he came back, he had two white tablets in his hand. Sitting down on the edge of the bed, he held them out to her. "Here," he said quietly, "take these."

She opened her eyes and looked at him, her eyes still glazed. "What are they?" she whispered.

He had a feeling that if he told her exactly what they were for, she would be absolutely mortified. She might be pretty brazen in bed and bold in her attitude, but she was also very modest. And if possible, he wanted to preserve that propriety for her. He smiled. "Just take 'em, okay? Trust me. They'll make you feel better."

Slowly she raised up on one elbow, took the two tablets and put them in her mouth, then accepted the glass of water. She took a drink and handed him back the glass, then lay down again, curling up as if she were cold. "I am sorry, Mitchell," she whispered, closing her eyes.

A funny feeling kicking in his chest, he pulled the comforter up under her chin, then bent down and brushed his mouth against her cheek. "Don't worry about it." Tucking back her hair, he straightened, the tightness in his chest getting worse. She was out cold in a matter of minutes, and he didn't know how long he stood there, watching her sleep. But it was a very long time before he could force himself to leave her. Even then, the feeling in his chest didn't go away.

Finally he went out to the kitchen and set the empty glass in the sink, then went to stand before the windows. Bracing his arm on the wide window frame, he stood staring out through the steady drizzle, his gaze fixed on the perennial gardens. No, their relationship hadn't been just about sex. He was terrified it was about something a whole lot more.

But there was even more to it than that. He felt as if something were slipping away from him, as if he were trying to hold on to a handful of very fine sand. And no matter how tightly he closed his fist, it continued to slip through his fingers. Why in hell was it so important to have her there in the mornings, and so imperative that he put her to bed in *his* bed? Maybe it was because the time they had together was also like sand, and it, too, was slowly slipping through his fingers.

Aware that his thoughts were taking him down a road he didn't want to travel, Mitch picked up his jacket and slipped it on, then fished his keys out of the pocket. She'd be out cold for at least a couple of hours, and with the rain, they weren't going to need him downstairs. Which meant he had time to go out and get some groceries and fix a decent dinner. He had never once cooked a meal for her, and it was about time he did. Besides, it would give him something to do to keep his mind off things.

It was just after seven when Maria finally appeared, her clothes rumpled and her hair a wild mess, the imprint of her hand still on her cheek. Although she still looked pretty out of it, the glassy look was gone from her eyes. She glanced from him to what he was doing, then hugged her arms around herself.

He shot her a quick look, then went back to slicing vegetables. "So you finally woke up."

She huddled in the warmth of her arms. "Yes," she said, her voice very soft.

He looked up at her again, an unsettling feeling fizzling through him when he saw how ill at ease she was. It was almost as if she was uncertain why she was there. Dismissing that thought, he went back to preparing their meal. "Dinner won't be ready for about half an hour. So if you want to grab a shower, I left towels for you on the counter in my bathroom."

She gave him a forced smile, then hugged herself tighter. "You do not have to make me dinner, Mitchell," she said, trying to drag up another smile. "I have—how do you say?—leftovers at home."

Keeping his expression shuttered, he scooped up the diced vegetables and dumped them in the simmering pot on the stove. A flicker of anger surfaced, but it was immediately extinguished by a sudden burst of insight. No wonder she was feeling unsure. Every other time she'd been in his apartment, they had immediately ended up in bed. He had never shown her the simple courtesy of a cooked meal, never had her over to watch a movie or even made her so much as a cup of coffee. Nor had he ever taken her anywhere special. His jaw hardened in self-disgust. No damned wonder she was acting uncertain.

And there wasn't a whole hell of a lot he could say to justify his rotten behavior. Keeping his face perfectly passive, he took a drink from the glass of red wine sitting on the counter, then set it down. "You're not eating leftovers, Maria. I'm making you dinner." She made a nervous gesture, then motioned toward the door. "I must go to my place first," she said, her tone very hushed. He nodded and started chopping a bundle of fresh parsley, wanting to stab the knife into the cutting board. The door closed behind her, and he slammed the knife down and turned away, jamming his hands on his hips as he tipped his head back. God, he could be such a jerk.

By the time she returned, he had the table set in the alcove overlooking the gardens. It had stopped raining, and he had opened one of the casement windows, letting in the smell of damp earth and wet lilacs. He heard her enter the kitchen, and he finished placing two wineglasses and the bottle of wine on the table before he glanced up.

She'd had a shower and was wearing something

long and loose, of a brightly woven fabric. Her hair was pulled back in a severe bun, and she looked as regal as a queen.

But she still had that hesitant look in her eyes, as if she didn't know quite what was expected of her. Mitch felt like a jerk all over again, and he knew he was going to have to do something to bridge the gap. He went over to her, and placing his hand along her jaw, he bent down and gave her a soft, undemanding kiss.

She abruptly caught his wrist, as if needing something to hold on to, and Mitch swore under his breath, truly hating himself.

Needing to reassure her, he gathered her up in a snug embrace and pressed his cheek against her still-damp hair. "Feeling better?"

Maria nodded and slipped her arms around his waist, and he felt her relax slightly. His expression sober, he rubbed his jaw against her temple, knowing somehow he had to erase that uncertain look from her eyes. "You hungry?"

She nodded again and turned her face against his.

He managed to drag up a smile. "Do you trust me?"

He heard a tiny trace of humor. "Yes."

"Well, just so you know. I haven't done any cooking for quite a while, so I'm gonna try really hard not to kill you tonight."

"It smells delicious."

Tucking her head against the curve of his neck, he cuddled her closer. "Don't let that fool you, kiddo. It doesn't mean a thing."

That finally got a real chuckle out of her. "I will try to be brave, Mitchell."

The meal went without a hitch, and during the course of it, Mitch got some insight into Maria's uncertainty. It made him feel a little awkward himself, having her sitting at his table and eating the dinner he had prepared for her, just as if it was an everyday occurrence.

But it wasn't an everyday occurrence. In fact, having a woman in his kitchen, having a woman at his table had never happened before. Up until Maria, he had never brought a woman here. He didn't think it was smart or appropriate—there were just some things you kept separate, especially with employees coming and going and family popping in and out. It was one rule he had never broken. He took his women elsewhere. He never brought them home. But he had brought Maria home.

Once he got her talking about Mexico, about the country and its people, they located a definite comfort zone. He had traveled there enough and had read enough that he had a pretty good grasp of the politics. And although he had never visited the specific area where she'd lived, he did have an understanding of the culture. But even so, he was a bit taken aback by her broad knowledge of the history. And he realized that his wife might not have had a privileged background, but she had managed to educate herself. And do it very well.

When he'd gone out for groceries, he had rented a couple of movies, and intended on just leaving the kitchen as it was after they finished dinner. But Maria wouldn't hear of it. So when she started clearing the table, he went along with her. It was kind of nice, having someone there, doing the routine things, talk-

ing about stuff. Like an ordinary husband and wife. If
that's what it took to make her feel comfortable, then
that was fine by him. Just as long as he had bridged
the gap. Just as long as she didn't start acting all hesitant and uncertain again.

They made it halfway through the first movie before
Maria started to really fade. She was curled up beside
him on his sofa, snuggled under a light throw, and at
some point, he had pulled her legs across his lap. He
remembered how one sister used to complain about
her legs aching, so he had started rubbing Maria's, and
the longer he rubbed, the heavier her eyelids got. He
was pretty sure she was trying to stay awake just to
be polite. Finding the remote control, he stopped the
movie and shut off the TV, then gave her leg a little
squeeze. "Let's give up on this and go to bed."

It was as if he'd dumped a bucket of cold water on
her. In a flash she was wide-awake, and she abruptly
withdrew her legs and sat up, curling them under her.
Avoiding looking at him, she began folding the throw,
and he could almost taste how uncomfortable she was.
Finally she spoke, gripping the folded blanket on her
lap. "I cannot..." She made a nervous gesture with
both hands. "I cannot sleep with you tonight, Mitchell," she said, her voice barely above a whisper. Then
she looked at him, her eyes dark with anxiety. "It is
not that I do not want—"

Catching her along the jaw with both hands, Mitch
pressed his thumbs against her mouth and smiled at
her. "I know, honey," he said, his voice husky. "And
that's okay." Having no intention of letting her spend
the night alone in her dark, empty apartment, he

leaned over and brushed a light kiss against her mouth. "Do you need anything from your place?"

She caught his arm, her breath giving a funny catch. "Yes."

He gave her another kiss. "Then go get what you need, and I'm going to close the windows in the kitchen. It's started raining again."

He was still in the kitchen, ostensibly putting away the last of the pots and pans, when she returned. The knot in his insides letting go, he turned out the light and met her in the entryway. She looked as uncertain as a schoolgirl, but he pretended not to notice. He did not want to make a big issue out of this.

Reaching around her, he turned the dead bolt on his door. He rarely locked it, but he was damned well going to lock it tonight. Sometimes his sisters didn't know the meaning of private, and the last thing he wanted was somebody walking in uninvited and unannounced. Draping his arm around Maria's shoulders, he led her down the hallway to the master bedroom.

Making sure he gave her as much time and privacy as she needed, he went into the bathroom and closed the door, then killed some time having a quick shower and equally quick shave.

When he came out, she was in bed, and he noticed that she had taken down her hair. Shutting the bedroom door, he turned off the light.

Mitch got a funny feeling in the vicinity of his heart as he climbed into bed. It was one of those times he felt very married to her. Stretching out, he slid his arm around her and drew her into his embrace. She resisted just a little, as if she wasn't sure what was expected of her. He tipped up her face and pressed a soft, gentling kiss against her mouth, then whispered, "It's okay. I just want to hold you."

Maria made a ragged little sound and abruptly turned toward him and came into his arms, holding on to him with a fierce strength. Nailed with a rush of raw emotion, Mitch closed his eyes and gathered her even closer, his jaw clenched. He'd been waiting for this all day—just to be able to hold her, to have her there beside him. He didn't care that this was as far as it could go. Maybe this was something he'd been missing all along—just taking time to relish the simple pleasure of holding her, of going to sleep in each other's arms.

She had on a big T-shirt, and Mitch ran his hand down her back, discovering that she also had panties on. He loved the feel of her skin.

"Mitchell?"

He rubbed the small of her back. "Hmm?"

"This is not upsetting for you?"

Holding the back of her head with his free hand, he pressed his mouth against her hair and gave her a reassuring squeeze. "No."

There was a slight pause, then she spoke again, her voice uneven. "I think you are not telling the truth," she whispered, almost as if she were on the verge of tears.

With a sharp jab of comprehension, Mitch came suddenly awake, the jolt turning to a sick, roiling sensation. And in the space of a heartbeat, he tapped into the source of her uncertainty. Plastered against him the way she was, she had to be aware that he was fully aroused, and she was feeling guilty, as if she were denying him his rights. He swallowed hard and closed his eyes, the churning feeling climbing higher. She was lying there, thinking she was doing something wrong, because she believed that the only value she had was as a bed partner. No wonder she was always gone in the morning.

He was so sickened by the realization, by the impressions he had left her with, it was all he could do to not launch himself out of bed. He deserved to be horsewhipped.

Forcing himself to set aside his self-disgust and focus on her—and to at least try to reassure her—he hugged her tighter, trying to find the right words. Exhaling heavily, he tucked his head against her. "Just because I'm aroused doesn't mean I have to have sex, Maria." He ran his hand down her back, pressing her even closer. "This feels pretty damned nice, too—just being able to hold you." He turned his head so his mouth was pressed against her forehead. "I like holding you."

She clutched his arm and took an unsteady breath. "I like it, too."

Feeling like a total jerk, he continued to massage the small of her back, trying to affirm her worth by touch alone. He remembered a long-ago incident, when his ex-wife had called him an insensitive clod, and he clenched his jaw, self-disgust rising up. She sure as hell had that right.

It was a long, long time before he fell asleep, and he was awakened at 4:00 a.m., when Maria tried to ease out of his hold. When he tightened his arms around her to keep her there, she whispered that she had to go to the bathroom. Reluctantly, he let her go. But he had turned on the light and was propped up on one elbow, waiting for her when she came out, making certain she didn't try to sneak away. He didn't want her leaving. And he didn't want her feeling she had denied or disappointed him in some way or another. He didn't like it that she had put so little value on herself. And that he had put so little value on her.

Mitch spent the entire weekend trying to make it up to her, but she was clearly not at ease in his apartment—he could see it in her body language and he could hear it in her voice. As soon as they were downstairs in the garden center, however, he could actually see her relax and return to normal. And she was the same old Maria, giving him a hard time at every turn.

It was as if in that setting she was sure of herself, as if she knew what her role was. Upstairs, she did not know. Except in the bedroom, where she held nothing back, and that realization bothered him more than anything. He didn't understand what was going on. And for some reason he didn't even try to untangle, he had started feeling tense and apprehensive, and he didn't understand that, either. It was as though he was standing on a narrow spit of land, and huge pieces were being washed away, destroying his foothold and leaving him nowhere to go.

He was almost glad when the campers returned. His association with Maria immediately returned to its old groove, and things got back to normal. Except they weren't really back to normal. Because there were times in the middle of the night, when he was alone, that he would get nailed by surges of panic, and he would lie there, his heart pounding, trying to contain it. He was falling apart, and he didn't even know why.

It got so bad, he couldn't stand himself. One day

he would be as testy as a wet wasp, then the very next day he would be practically incapacitated by dread. Other times he felt as if he were operating several feet off the ground. Nothing made sense. The only times that were consistent were those nights with Maria, when she was there with him; then he would feel half-way whole. But then morning would come and she would be gone, and the cycle would start all over again.

A gut-deep fear started to set in, and more than once, he found himself out in the compound, moving bags of lawn fertilizer, at three in the morning. It was as if his spit of land was disintegrating so fast, he was constantly scrambling to keep his feet under him. It finally got so bad that he started to avoid her, and he'd spend nights in his office, drafting landscape plans, trying to hold the panic at bay. It didn't take long for Maria to pick up on the signals, and he could see the sparkle go out of her eyes.

He felt so damned guilty about what he'd done to her that he couldn't even look her in the eye. And it started to eat at him, knowing he was still jerking her around. He knew it, and he sensed she knew it, too. He was a total bastard for how he had misused her values, and he felt even worse because he knew he was the cause of the new shadows of unhappiness he could see in her face. And as much as he hated what he was doing, he couldn't seem to stop himself.

It all came to a head one evening, just at dusk, when he was out rearranging inventory in the shrub and tree lot. He was consolidating the different species of hon-eysuckle, and had two pots in his hands when she appeared on the gravel path, her arms folded in front of her, her face drawn with strain. She reached out and touched the leaves on the shrub by the gate, then abruptly folded her arms again. She spoke, not quite meeting his gaze. "I have made a call to Mr. Peterson," she said, her voice as strained as her expression, "to find out the regulation concerning the length of marriage. I thought you should know."

Taking a deep breath, Mitch set the shrubs down, then stripped off his gloves. Mr. Peterson was the immigration lawyer, and Mitch wasn't so thick that he didn't get the message. She was redefining the arrangement. And he knew he had this coming. A hard knot settled in his stomach, and he had to brace himself against the dark, cold feeling. "Fine."

"I will tell you when I know."

Resting his hands on his hips, he finally looked at her. "You do whatever you want," he said, his voice flat.

She held his gaze a moment, then turned to go.

His hands still on his hips, Mitch stared down at the ground, an awful hollow feeling climbing up his chest. He had screwed things up before in his life, but never like this. Never.

"Mitchell."

He lifted his head. She was standing by the gate, the mauve and flame-red sky behind her. She stared at him, her expression obscured by shadows. "I am sorry, Mitchell," she said, her voice very quiet.

The hollow feeling settled squarely in the middle of his chest, and it hurt like hell to breathe. He clenched his jaw against the feeling, then tipped his head. "So am I."

Without any indication she'd heard him, she turned

and walked away, and Mitch remained where he was, hating himself. Only it was worse than just hating himself. It felt as if every speck of light in his life had just been extinguished. And he was left standing alone in the dark.

The next few days were bleak. Nothing seemed to ease the scouring sense of loss—not every backbreaking job he could think of, not plowing through mind-numbing paperwork, not five-kilometer runs in the middle of the night. And during those nights when he did manage to fall asleep, the tormenting dreams came back, only now they had changed. They had become bleak and empty and filled with such aloneness it was as if he were the only person left on earth.

After a few days of that, he was so numb with exhaustion he could barely function. It rained again, another real downpour, and he had to quit working. Feeling as if he had finally hit the wall, he came home, had a quick shower and fell into bed, certain there would be no dreams tonight.

But he was wrong. There was another one, but this one was different. This one was so vivid, it was as if Maria were there, warm and solid in his arms. The soft, soft kiss was so real he could taste her, and his senses flooded with the scent of gardenias. His body responded and he groaned, losing himself in the heat of her, the rush of blood to his groin making him hard and erect. And the kiss went on, and her hands—her hands were everywhere, taking him to the very edge.

Suddenly there was nothing—no taste, no touch— and the dream contracted and shrank into a pinpoint of color, and he struggled against the awful loss. But before he could call out, a tight, wet heat gloved him and a weight settled on his hips. He groaned and arched up against it, so close, so close to release.

His heart pounding, he came abruptly awake, realizing it was no dream. It was real—she was real—and he was hit with such a surge of relief, it swept him under. His face contorting with another rush of emotion, he crushed her against him, hanging on to her like a lifeline.

Desperate to assure himself of the reality, he jammed his hand into her hair and dragged her head down, covering her mouth in a hard, bruising kiss that set off a new wave of desperation. Whispering his name, Maria responded, holding nothing back, and every caress, every touch nearly stripped him raw.

He reached the final climax, but before he had a chance to recover his strength or his senses, she was gone. And he was left alone in the dark, the emptiness so intense, it was as if she had ripped his heart right out of his chest.

It was a hell of a way to say goodbye.

It had been bad before. But it was ten times worse after. Mitch had never felt so terrified and defenseless in his entire life. It was as if her withdrawal stripped away every protective shield he had developed, and he was left naked and defenseless. He didn't like the feeling. He didn't like it one bit. He had nowhere to go. Nothing seemed to line up anymore.

And it didn't get any better. It was as if he had developed some weird internal radar, and he sensed her everywhere. The awful hollow feeling was bad enough, but what damned near killed him were the lengths she went to avoid him. And he knew better than anyone how trapped she was. Unless she confided in his family, she had no one to turn to. And nowhere else to go. If she wanted to keep her family in Canada, she had to play out the charade. Because their livelihood and well-being depended on her.

Realizing it couldn't go on the way it was and knowing he was the only one who could take the pressure off her, he decided to clear out for a few days. It was the only thing he could think of that would give them both some breathing room. And God knew, he needed some time to get his head together.

With that intent in mind, Mitch spent the last Thursday in June making arrangements for his crew foreman to handle the contract jobs, and making sure there were no loose ends. He had nailed everything down except one piece of business he had to take care of. He knew he owed a supplier for several loads of loam that had been delivered to one of the landscaping sites, but was damned if he could find the invoice.

Feeling a headache coming on, he leaned back in his chair and rubbed his eyes, wearily wondering when all the emotional upheaval was going to stop.

Heaving a tired sigh, he got up and headed for the stairs. Jordan was around somewhere. Maybe she had already dealt with the damned invoice.

She wasn't at the checkout area, nor was she in the staff room. So he headed through the tropical greenhouse, figuring she might be with Doris. He was just about to enter the second greenhouse when he caught a glimpse of Maria that made him stop dead in his tracks.

She was standing by the racks of blooming annuals with Wanda David, who had her hand resting on the canopy of a stroller. Wanda was one of his regular customers, and the last time Mitch had seen her, she had been very, very pregnant. But from the fit of her shorts and T-shirt, she was definitely not pregnant anymore.

Maria crouched down in front of the stroller, her face suddenly alight with such awe and delight, it made his heart clench up into a tight little ball.

"He is beautiful," she breathed, reaching inside. "And so much hair."

Wanda went around to the front of the stroller and bent over, lifting out a tiny bundle. "Well, you're just going to have to hold him, Maria." She grinned and placed the baby in Maria's arms. "He won't know he's being properly adored unless you hold him." She pushed the stroller to one side. "And since you have him, I'm going to get some more begonias. Mine got beaten to death in the last downpour."

Her face aglow with heart-stopping reverence, Maria carefully cuddled the tiny sleeping infant in her arms and folded back the light receiving blanket. "You are such a little one," she whispered, tracing her finger down his tiny cheek. "And so beautiful." The baby made a face and squirmed, and Maria gave a soft laugh and lifted him up, turning him slightly as she nestled him against her shoulder. Then she closed her eyes and began to sway with him, her hand cupping his head, an expression of such longing on her face that even a blind man would know she had an unsatisfied ache in her heart.

It was the look on her face that did him in—the heart-wrenching tenderness, the terrible longing. It didn't take a genius to see how much she ached for a child of her own. And in that instant, everything Mitch believed—or wanted to believe—came crashing down. He saw his life for what it really was, and experienced such a wrenching sense of loss, it was almost more than he could handle.

His vision suddenly blurring, he turned and walked away, the suffocating ache in his chest nearly incapacitating him. God. He had been such a damned fool.

He nearly ran Jordan down as he rounded the corner on his way to the stairs. She caught his arm, her eyes widening with alarm. "Mitch. What's the matter?"

He tried to speak, but his throat was too tight, and he looked away and shook his head.

Her expression awash with compassion, she took his stiff face between her hands, her gaze dark with understanding. "Oh, Mitchell," she whispered.

He pulled her hands away and gave them a squeeze. His voice was so strained, it didn't even sound like his own. "I'm heading out of town for a few days. You can reach me on my cell phone if you need me."

Feeling as if his face was going to crack, he walked away, barely able to see. Man, he had screwed up before. But he had never screwed up like this. This time he had lost the chance of a lifetime.

Chapter 9

His first line of escape had always been to head for the tree farm, but his site manager would be there, and Mitch could not stomach the thought of having to be civil to anyone. He needed some space, but most of all, he needed to be alone. So he got in his Jeep and started driving in the opposite direction.

At first, the only thing in his head was an endless loop of images, images of Maria and that baby. And every time the image of her face flashed in his mind, when she had cuddled that tiny being against her breast, his throat would cramp and he'd get such a hell of an ache in his chest it would just about do him in. He had been so blind. He had been such a bastard.

Then the guilt would set in, and he'd recall every detail of that weekend together, how ill at ease she had been in his kitchen, at his table, as if she was in the wrong place and had no business being there. He had kidded himself that it hadn't been just about sex, but that was exactly what it had been about. He had never even had the decency to sit down and think about the consequences from her point of view, about how she must be feeling. Or the role she was playing. All he had thought about was how much he wanted her and his own gratification.

And where in hell did that leave her? To the world, she was his wife. But because of the deal, that was not how she saw herself. He spent a lot of time wondering just how badly he'd hurt her with his callousness. He had never stopped to consider. Not once.

Yeah, he had offered her sanctuary. And that would have been great, if only he had kept his hands to himself. But he hadn't been able to do that, and he'd been the one to breach the boundaries. And now she was the one paying the price.

No, he had never once stopped to think how this was going to affect her. He had rationalized. And he had compartmentalized. He'd made damned sure he made no real emotional investment. And he'd pretty much left her out there, flapping in the breeze. He had been so busy protecting himself, making sure he didn't get hurt, that he had never really stopped to think what he was doing to her.

Mitch drove for miles, trying to outrun his personal demons. Wanting to avoid the U.S. border, he headed east, picking up secondary highways that took him into the flat, endless stretches of prairie. Those vast empty spaces seemed to echo the growing emptiness inside him. He felt as if he was dying inside.

It was dark when he finally recognized that he was operating on nothing but sheer stupidity and dumb luck, and that he was an accident just waiting to happen. Feeling as if he didn't have an ounce of life left in him, he pulled into some Podunk prairie town that had one motel with a restaurant, a saloon in a rundown hotel and a gas station that was still open.

The gas station was a necessity, but the saloon and the motel were simply conveniences. Realizing that he was pretty much running on empty himself, he decided to pack it in for the night. Because no matter how far he drove or how many roads he took, there was no way he could get away from what was chasing him. The pain and the shame were all trapped inside him, and there was only one way he could exorcise them, at least for a few hours. So after he gassed up and got a room in the motel, he hit the saloon. By midnight, he wasn't feeling much of anything. The last thing he remembered was trying to unlock the door of his room, then nothing. Just deep dark blackness that swallowed him up.

When he came to the next morning, he couldn't get his bearings. He didn't have a clue where he was. And it wasn't until he was in the truck and checked the map that he found out. One thing for sure, he had a hangover to end all hangovers. And a headache that no medication would touch. Since his eyes felt as if someone was stabbing hot pokers into them when he looked into the sun, he did himself a favor and headed north.

He was in so much physical agony, he didn't think about much of anything all morning, except keeping the gas pedal down and staying between the ditches. Finally he found an unused approach to a wheat field, parked the Jeep, rolled down the windows and crashed for an hour. When he woke up, he found another little town and finally got something to eat. His stomach wasn't too sure it liked the idea of actually having food down there, but he felt almost human after. Almost.

Which was not necessarily a good thing. As soon as the headache faded, he kept replaying things over and over in his head. And that awful hollow feeling came back, only this time a hundred times worse. He had to face up to some facts, one of which was the hard, cold reality that he had hurt her. He hadn't meant to, but he had. And he had used her. For that alone he deserved to be horsewhipped.

It wasn't until that night, in another dreary motel in another nameless prairie town, that he finally faced another truth. As hard as it was to drop all his defenses, as hard as it was to stand stripped naked of any pretenses, he had to come to grips with the fact that he was head-over-heels in love with her.

He didn't even know when it had happened— maybe right from the moment he'd first laid eyes on her in the airport. When he'd got lost in her eyes. But somewhere along the line, he had fallen—and fallen hard. And it was not an easy, gentle kind of love. No, this was the gut-deep, soul-shattering kind that could hold a man together, no matter how grim, how ugly, how unspeakable the circumstances—or could tear him to pieces. It was the kind of love that could bring a man to his knees.

And he finally had to own up to something else. All these years he had been playing games with himself. He had never admitted to anyone, even himself, how the failure of his first marriage had nearly destroyed him. He had covered those feelings up and buried them deep, and he'd never let himself get so close to a woman that he could ever get burned that way again.

His family was right—he had turned into a workaholic and a recluse. Because he had made up his mind that he just wasn't going to take that kind of chance again. But then he'd got trapped in his own stupid defense system, and it wasn't Maria that had tripped him up. He'd done that all by himself. And whatever chance he might have had with her was now so badly mangled, he could never make it right. There was no such thing as a second chance.

By day five, Mitch was sure he'd been down every damned country road in three provinces, and he felt pretty much like death on wheels. He might have run hundreds of miles away from home, but as far as self-discovery was concerned, he had only managed baby steps. And he sure as hell hadn't made a miraculous discovery of the way out of the maze. But no matter how much soul-searching he did, some things remained constant—he was a bastard, he had screwed up and he was so much in love with his wife it was as if someone had ripped the heart right out of him.

He also knew he couldn't keep running. At some point, he was going to have to turn the Jeep around and go back and face her.

That night he found another seedy little motel, and if he felt like hell, one look in the cracked mirror told him he looked even worse. Bloodshot eyes, hollowed out cheeks, a five-day growth of beard—he was pretty pathetic. Forcing himself to pull it together, he had a long hot shower and even shaved, then stretched out on the bed and faced one more fact. Somehow, he was going to have to get along without her.

His chest jamming up with a crippling sense of loss, he draped his arm over his eyes and swallowed hard. He wasn't sure he could do it. It would tear him to shreds, and he had no place left to hide. But it didn't matter, because he knew there was no way in hell he could ever hide from this loss.

He awoke several hours later, his heart pounding, his chest so tight he could barely breathe. But it wasn't fear clamping down on him—it was a heightened sense of awareness. And another fact hit him square in the face.

That night when she had come to him in the darkness, when they'd started making love before he was even fully awake, there had been no protection. Nothing. Just them. Skin to skin.

Feeling as if he'd just got a jolt of electricity, Mitch hit the floor pacing, his heart pounding. From the weekend when she'd been feeling so rotten till that night—how many days was it? A crazy kind of hope started zipping through him, and he made three circuits around the room.

He recalled in vivid detail the look on her face when she'd held that newborn, as if she'd been praying. Holy hell! What if she'd been hoping to get pregnant? What would that mean?

Did it mean she *wanted* to have his baby? A crazy lightness surged up in his chest, and Mitch closed his eyes, a giddy sensation making his head swim. Damn. Maybe. Just maybe.

He glanced at his watch—2:13 a.m. If he drove like hell, stopped only for gas and broke a few speed limits, he could be home in eighteen hours. Hope warring with the voice of caution, he started throwing his stuff into his small duffel bag. Thank God he had paid for the night when he checked in, and had paid cash. Because he was getting the hell out of there, and he was getting out now.

It wasn't until he'd been on the road a couple of hours that it hit him—if he was right and she had tried to get pregnant, it meant she was planning on cutting out. Because there was no way she'd stick around and have that baby while she was still in Calgary. No way. She would never draw his family into that kind of situation. Never. If she had gotten pregnant, she would take off.

Fear raised its ugly head, and Mitch jammed his foot down on the accelerator, fighting to stay calm. It didn't matter if she did cut and run. He'd track her down. There was no way he was letting her go. But the fear hung in there, keeping him wide-awake and focused.

Mitch pulled into the parking lot of his garden center exactly seventeen hours later, so strung out on too much coffee, no sleep and a whole lot of dread, he was prepared to rip hinges off. He strode into the garden center, crossed the checkout area and was just headed for the stairs when he heard footsteps behind him.

"Mitch. Will you stop, please?"

Clenching his jaw to control the feeling racing around in his chest, he turned. Jordan hurried over to him, worry in her eyes. "Thank God you're home. I've been trying to raise you for three days on your cell phone."

Alarm gave his heart a shot of adrenaline, and he stared at his sister-in-law, trying to stay calm. His tone was harsh and to the point. "What's wrong?"

Jordan also got right to the point. "There was a phone call a couple of days ago for Mrs. Munroe, so Doris put it through to me. It was a travel agent, with quotes for flights to Mexico."

His stomach suddenly sitting in his shoes, Mitch asked the question he dreaded asking. "Is she gone?"

Her face etched with worry, Jordan shook her head. "No. At least she wasn't. She was here this afternoon."

His face feeling like it had been hacked out of granite, Mitch clamped his teeth together and started toward the stairs. He clenched and unclenched his fists. Too close. Far too close.

And maybe too late.

He pounded on her apartment door and got no response, and considered barging in. But just as he made up his mind to do it, the fire door opened and Roberto sauntered through, his face breaking into a big grin when he saw Mitch. "Mitchell. You are back."

Holding down the crazy mix of panic, fear, urgency and hope, Mitch forced himself to relax his stance, but it took every ounce of control he had not to bark at the kid. "Where's your mother?"

A small frown appearing, Roberto shrugged. "She has gone to seven o'clock Mass."

It was a toss-up. Did he go after her or did he wait for her to get home? If he went after her, there was a good chance he would miss her. And if he missed her at this time of night, it would take her at least an hour to get home on the bus. There was no way, feeling like he was, that he could wait another hour.

He went after her.

The summer sun had settled low in the west by the time Mitch reached the church, the sharp angle casting long shadows against the trees along the boulevard. The church lot was full and he had to park on the street. He knew he had no business going in, but there was no way he could stay outside and wait for her. No way on God's green earth. If he didn't lay eyes on her pretty soon, he was going to climb right out of his skin.

It was a big church, and Mitch was nearly halfway down the side aisle before he spotted her. She was kneeling, her head bent, and even from a distance he could see the rosary in her hand. She had on a simple white blouse with her hair tied back with a dark ribbon, and he didn't think he had ever seen her look more beautiful.

For the first time in hours, he felt as if he could draw a proper breath, and his heart rate finally started to slow down. As he watched from across the rows of pews, she lifted the rosary and kissed the cross, and Mitch closed his eyes for a second as another band of tension let go. He had found her, she was safe and that was all he cared about. He didn't care what protocol he was breaking, or how impolite it was to stand there with the service going on; he was not moving an inch. And he wasn't taking his eyes off her.

Leaning back against the wall, he folded his arms, the panic finally easing off. He didn't have a clue what he was going to say to her; he just hoped to hell there was some truth to his speculations. That maybe she had come to him that night with the hope of getting pregnant. That maybe, just maybe, she cared a little bit about him. Because he didn't know how he would handle it if he was wrong.

By the time the service ended, Mitch was back on the treadmill again, with a whole lot of self-doubt giving him no end of grief. He was in such a mess he had just about convinced himself that he may as well cut his losses and go home. But then she turned to leave, and he got a good look at her face. And a new surge of hope overrode everything else. She looked worse than he did.

Moving quickly through a row of empty pews, he caught up to her as she waited to merge with the stream of departing parishioners. It wasn't until he was within arm's reach that Mitch realized Enrico and Grandfather Rodriquez were directly in front of her.

Damn it all to hell, that was something he hadn't planned on. He'd figured he'd just catch her by the arm and march her out of there, then take her somewhere private.

Okay. So they were here, and he had to change his strategy. It was no big deal. It just meant he would have to wait until they got back home before he got her alone. If she didn't tell him to go straight to hell first.

Stepping into the aisle beside her, he grasped her elbow, his pulse going crazy the minute he touched her.

Trying to pull her arm free, she looked up, her expression freezing when she saw who it was. But it was he disbelief he saw there that nearly killed him, and he guarded expression as wariness took over. It took

her a couple of minutes to get her wits about her, ther
she lifted her arm, trying to break his hold. Looking
straight ahead, she continued to resist. "I do not war
to see you, Mitchell."

He could see for himself what he had done to her
and his stomach did such a rollover, he almost fer
sick. God, he had been such a first-class heel. Trying
to ease the awful feeling, he slid his hand down he
arm and grasped her hand. His voice was tense wher
he answered. "Too bad. I've come to take you home."

She stared at him a moment, her expression fixec
and unreadable; then she abruptly faced forward, he
body taut. It was pretty obvious she was over the
shock of seeing him there, and was now determinec
to shut him out. The only thing that gave him any hope
at all was the way she stumbled against the last pew
as if she couldn't see where she was going.

It wasn't until they got outside that Grandfather anc
Enrico realized Mitch had come for them, and Mitc
decided it was probably a good thing that they wer
there. Because as far as Maria was concerned, he
wasn't. Hell, she was so remote, it was almost as i
she wasn't there, either.

She pulled out of his grasp when they reached hi
Jeep, and without giving him a chance to interfere, sh
climbed in the back with Enrico, her face like ston
as she sat staring straight ahead.

Enrico kept up a string of chatter all the way home
and Mitchell was damned grateful he did. It woul
have been a pretty grim ride back otherwise.

If it had been tense in the Jeep, it was even wors
when they arrived home. Maria tried to get out ahea
of everybody, but the old man cut her off, and Mitc

was able to nab her. He grabbed her by the upper arm, making sure she didn't get a second chance. His nerves were shot, his stomach was in knots and he was so totally road whipped that he simply didn't have a whole lot of patience left. Not about to give her another chance to cut and run, he tightened his hold so she couldn't twist free when they reached his door. She tried anyway, and Mitch yanked her back. "Don't fight me, Maria," he snapped.

Acting blind and deaf to the silent battle of wills going on behind him, Grandfather Rodriguez shooed Enrico into their apartment with both hands, as if he were herding a flock of goats. Mitch waited until the door closed behind the two, then opened his own door. There was another tug of war, and she tried to break his hold. Then she tried to grab the door frame, but he pried her fingers off and ended up practically shoving her into his apartment. Once inside, he locked the door and leaned back against it, not sure what in hell to do now. She whirled away from him and started toward the kitchen, and the irritation drained right out of him. Resting his head against the door, he closed his eyes, not knowing what to say, but knowing he had to say something. His heart started to race with fear, and he didn't know what he would do if this didn't work. He didn't know what in hell he would do.

His face feeling like granite, he straightened and opened his eyes, his voice rough with emotion when he spoke. "I need to talk to you, Maria."

She whirled and came back into the hall, temper blazing in her eyes, her body trembling with fury as she jammed her hands on her hips. "Well, I do not

need to talk to you, Mitchell,'' she shouted, her voic
shaking. Rage building, she pointed her finger at him
''You leave without speaking one word, and no on
tells me where you are. I wonder if you are dead.'
Tears welled in her eyes, and she threw up her hands
''What did I do that was so wrong you had to leave?'

She stopped and abruptly covered her face with he
hands, and a low sob was wrenched from her. Fo
some reason, her fury swept away whatever doubts h
had left, and a sudden weakness fizzled through hin
It was a good sign she was crying. A very good sigr

The sound of her absolute misery gave him th
strength to move, and he straightened and went to he
Feeling as if his chest was too tight to accommodat
his pounding heart, he caught her and pulled her int
his arms, wrapping her up in a fierce embrace. Sh
tried to fight him but he held her fast, feeling aliv
and whole for the first time in days. Thank God sh
was furious. He didn't know what he would have don
if she had remained cold and distant.

Sobbing and trying to twist free, she pressed he
fists against his chest, trying to break his hold. Bu
Mitch simply trapped her hands and hung on to he
realizing one more thing about his wife. If she didn
care, she wouldn't be fighting him. And another rev
elation hit. If she didn't care, she never would hav
gone to bed with him in the first place. Never in
million years.

She twisted against him again, and his whole bod
responded. With his jaw clenched against the agoni
ing pleasure of holding her again, Mitch closed h
eyes, loving her so much his body couldn't hold it al
Locking her against him, he tucked his head again

hers, so many emotions for her breaking loose it felt
as if his chest might crack wide open. His throat so
full he couldn't even swallow, he pressed his mouth
against her temple. "I love you, Maria," he whispered
roughly. "It wasn't supposed to happen, and I fought
it like hell, but it happened anyway." Drawing a deep,
shaky breath, he prayed to God he had the words to
make things right. He kissed her again, his voice uneven as he whispered against her hair. "You terrify
me, because you hold my whole life in your hands."

She went so still, so perfectly still it was like he
had a statue in his arms; then she jerked her head back,
her face wet with tears, a look of absolute shock in
her eyes. She stared at him, then her eyes filled with
tears again. "You love me?" she whispered.

He gave her a little smile, his heart doing flip-flops
in his chest. "Oh, yeah," he said gruffly. "I love
you."

Tears caught in her long lashes as she stared up at
him, her body trembling again. "You are sure?"

His expression softening, he used his thumb to wipe
away the tears. He smiled again. "Absolutely sure."

She stared at him an instant longer, then another
sob broke loose as she grabbed his face. "I am going
to kill you, Mitchell, for scaring me so." Muttering
something in Spanish, she pulled his head down and
kissed him. It was the kind of kiss that was meant to
incite and ignite, and it absolutely rocked him. It set
off such a chain reaction, he went a little crazy.

He tried to be gentle, but she would have none of
it. And he tried to hold back, but she was not having
any of that, either. It was like two supernovas collid-
ing. Like a war—a war with all defenses blasted to

smithereens, with nothing left to hide behind. A war of desperation, of frenzied urgency and need—a hot, frantic, driving kind of need that lifted him higher and carried him further than anything he had ever experienced before. And she was surely killing him, because that was exactly what would happen if he had to stop.

But Maria didn't have stopping in mind. Her mouth welding against his, she yanked at his clothes, and whatever control Mitch had left got incinerated right there. This wasn't about sex. This was about surviving. This was about joining two halves into one unbelievable whole.

Fighting with her clothes, he finally got rid of all the barriers, and he lifted her up and jammed her against the wall, and she locked her legs around him. She sobbed against his mouth as he thrust into her, and he felt her nails rake his back. His face contorting, he thrust into her again, and she stiffened and arched back, her fingers digging into his shoulders.

A blinding storm carried and drove him on, like wild waves crashing together, and Mitch hung on to her and rode it out, loving her totally. Loving her with all that he was and with everything he had in him.

His release was cataclysmic, torn from every cell in his body, and he crushed her against him when she cried out and convulsed around him, her climax sending him over the edge. Twisting his face against her neck, he hung on, his own release going on and on wringing him dry.

It was like nothing he had ever experienced before. It cleansed him. It restored him. And he felt as if he had just been reborn.

Her whole body trembling, Maria collapsed around

him, hanging on to him so tightly he didn't know where she left off and he began. Spanning the back of her head with his hand, he tightened his hold even more, wishing he could draw her right inside him.

Locking her against him, he stood there with her weight braced against the wall, so weak and so spent even his legs were trembling. It took a while before he could marshal any strength at all. Pressing her head against his, he locked his other arm around her hips, then stepped out of the wad of clothing around his feet. His hold fierce and protective, he turned and carried her down the hallway to his bedroom.

Knowing there was absolutely no way he could let her go, he sat down on the edge of the bed with her clinging to him like a leech. His breathing still a little ragged, he turned his head and kissed her neck. "Take my shirt off, love," he whispered, his voice very gruff. "I don't want to let you go."

Tightening her legs around his waist, she eased away, and with some fumbling, they got rid of his shirt. It was easier with her, but she kept her eyes closed when he pulled her blouse off, and the instant her arms were free, she folded into him, holding on with a desperate strength. With one arm braced on the bed and the other holding her, he shifted his weight and lay down with her on top of him, their bodies still joined together.

Unable to contain the feeling, Mitch let out a hoarse groan as she settled on him, taking him in even deeper.

Knowing he had been brutally rough with her, he kissed her with infinite care, then began stroking her back, trying to soothe her, needing to give her some gentleness.

She abruptly twisted her face into the curve of his neck, and that one small gesture nearly did him in. Pressing her head tighter against him, he closed his eyes. "You will never know how much I need you in my life, Maria," he said, his voice uneven. "You're a miracle I never expected to happen."

He didn't think it was possible, but she held him even tighter. Then, with a shuddering sob, she turned her head and found his mouth, and any doubts he might have had disappeared like smoke. She had forgiven him. He could wait for the words. Her response told him all he needed to know. And he gave himself up to the miracle of her.

The second time was slower, softer, longer. Much, much longer, but the final outcome was the same, and Mitch's senses were incinerated by her. It took him a long time to come down from that high, and it took even longer for him to get any strength back. And she still hadn't said a single word since he had carried her to bed.

Finally able to move, he rolled onto his back, taking her with him.

Lying flat, he snuggled her against him, then drew her head onto his shoulder, giving her a tight hug. Mitch smiled to himself and slowly combed his fingers through her hair. God, he felt as if he didn't have a whole bone left in his body.

Mustering up a tiny bit of energy, he tipped his chin and kissed the top of her head. "Just so you know. There's no way in hell I'm letting you go."

He felt her breath catch; then she finally spoke, a funny little tremor of uncertainty in her voice. "You are sure, Mitchell?"

He grinned and gave her an emphatic answer. "Oh, yeah. I'm sure."

As if a little short on strength herself, she propped herself on one elbow and looked at him, doubt darkening her eyes. "I am not convinced," she whispered.

He pulled her head down and gave her a soft, reassuring kiss, then he nestled her head back against the curve of his shoulder. "I don't blame you. Especially when I've been acting like such a jerk."

"You are not a jerk," she interjected, her tone defensive.

Amusement softened his expression, and he gave her a little squeeze. "Yeah, I was." His expression sobering, he let out a heavy sigh. "I've been building defenses for a long time—a very long time. I was going to make damned sure I never let anyone get close enough to hurt me again." He sighed once more and smoothed her hair back, brushing another kiss against her forehead. His voice was very quiet as he tried to explain. "I thought I was getting on with my life, but what I was really doing was hiding. But I had to drive a lot of miles and do a whole lot of soul-searching before I could admit that to myself." Needing to reassure her, he ran his hand up her naked back, then kissed her again. "You scared the hell out of me," he whispered. "Because I knew you could turn my life upside down."

As if unable to hold all the hurt any longer, she started to cry again, and she curled into him. "I was so afraid I had lost you."

His own vision getting a little misty, Mitch closed his eyes and hugged her hard. "You aren't going to lose me, Maria. Because there's no way I'm ever letting you go.''

''You are telling the truth?''

''The absolute truth.''

He let her cry it out, then he used the heel of his hand to dry her tears. His chest full, he drew her closer. ''Marry me, Maria.''

She went very still, then took a deep, tremulous breath. ''We are already married.''

Caressing her back, he stared at the ceiling. ''Not the way you deserve to be married. In a church, with a priest.''

She pulled out of his arms and sat up, using his shirt to wipe her eyes; then she slipped it on and hugged it around her. Finally she looked at him, her eyes filling up again. ''I don't want another marriage,'' she whispered.

Shoving his hand under his head to keep from pulling her back down, Mitch frowned. ''Why not?''

Avoiding his gaze, she gave a little shrug. ''Because I like the one I had.''

That didn't seem like a real answer, and she was trying very hard to avoid his gaze. Catching her under the chin, he forced her head up so he could see her face. ''Why, Maria?''

She looked at him, then looked down and began drawing lines on his biceps with her fingernail. It was a while before she answered. ''I went to see a priest before we were married. Did you know that?''

His attention riveted on her, he used his thumb to wipe away another track of tears. ''No.''

Catching his hand, she laced her fingers through his and gripped it tightly. ''I thought it was wrong, this marriage of agreement. He listened to me. Then he asked me if I loved you.'' She swallowed hard, then finally lifted her head and looked at him, her heart in her eyes. ''I said I did, that I loved you very much.''

Mitch closed his eyes and let his breath go in a rush. Thank God. Thank God. Catching her by the back of the head, he dragged her back down into his arms. Trying to get his mind around what she had just told him, he hugged her hard, his heart pounding, his mind swimming with an unbelievable high. She loved him. Even back then, she knew she loved him.

Caressing his neck with the tips of her fingers, she placed a soft kiss on the underside of his jaw. ''So that is why I do not want another marriage, Mitchell,'' she whispered unevenly. ''I want to keep the one I had.''

''Ah, Maria,'' he whispered hoarsely. ''What did I ever do to deserve you?''

She gave him a firm hug, then chuckled. ''Many bad things, I am guessing. I am no prize, Mitchell.''

Feeling as if she had just handed him the world, he hugged her back. ''Ah. But you are.''

Pulling out of his embrace, she sat up and looked down at him, the front of his shirt gaping open. There was a stubborn glint in her eye. ''No, I am not, Mitchell. I am very, how you say, aggravating. And I have a terrible temper. I will make your life miserable.''

Transfused with a sensation that was lighter than air, Mitch felt every knot in his belly let go. And suddenly he needed to tease her. Once again sliding one hand under his head, he reached up and fingered her hair, absolutely straight-faced. ''I never noticed.''

She grinned and smacked his hand. ''You are a very

bad liar, Mitchell. You get this twinkle in your eyes when you tell lies.'' Her expression suddenly sobering, she caught his hand and grasped it between both of hers. ''I have something else to confess to you.'' She traced the vein in the back of his hand, then swallowed hard and looked at him. ''That night. When I came to you—I was not careful, Mitchell.''

Aware of how anxious she was, he locked his thumb across hers. He figured they'd both had about as much heavy stuff as they could handle for one night. He stroked her palm and grinned. ''I know.''

She glared at him. ''You know?''

His grin softening into a smile, he let go of her hand and brushed his knuckles along her jaw. ''Yeah. But I'd like you to tell me why.''

She studied him a moment, as if deciding whether to comply or not, then she looked away. ''I thought what we shared was finished,'' she said, her voice very soft. ''And I would have to go back to my home. But,'' she said, her voice turning into a whisper, ''I wanted to take your baby with me.''

Nailed with another heavy-duty reaction, Mitch caught her under the chin and lifted her face, feeling as if she'd just launched a weather balloon in his chest. Holding her gaze, he stroked her bottom lip with his thumb. ''I'll give you a baby whenever you want. And as many as you want.'' Trying to get some air past the fullness in his chest, he caressed her lip again. ''So are you?''

Her eyes dark and solemn, she shook her head.

Jackknifing up, he clasped her face and gave her a hard, wet kiss; then he lay back down, bringing her with him. Tucking her head against his, he snuggled her deeper into his embrace and started combing his fingers through her hair. "I'd like a bit more time with just the two of us," he said gruffly, "but if you get pregnant from what happened here today, I'm not going to be the least bit unhappy about it." Realizing things could get very emotional again, he decided to rile her. He grinned. "My plan is to keep you barefoot and pregnant."

Her head came up and she gave him a sharp jab in the ribs, her eyes flashing. "I do not think so, Mitchell." Then, realizing he was baiting her, she pinched his arm. "You are a very, very bad husband. You like to prick my temper."

He ran his hand up her arm and gave her neck a squeeze. "Yes I do."

She slanted a scolding look down at him, then gave a little shiver, and goose bumps sprang up on her arms. Rolling away from her, he reached down to snag the sheet, and she gave a horrified gasp and placed her hand on his shoulder. "Oh, Mitchell," she whispered, "look what I have done to your back."

Yanking the sheet up, he pulled her back down into his embrace. Dragging her under him, he trapped her legs between his and grinned, then leaned down and kissed her mouth. "Now you will have to keep me. I'm damaged goods."

She touched his face, love and amusement shining in her eyes. "I will keep you," she teased. "It is part of our marriage of agreement."

He lowered his head and kissed her again, liking the way she went all soft and yielding in his arms.

This was no marriage of agreement. This was some kind of miracle.

Epilogue

The thick stand of trees along the creek was vivid with autumn colors, the aspen and birch draped in gold, the underbrush spattered with the reds and magentas of wild roses and chokecherry bushes. And beneath the trees, the wild grasses had turned rust and bronze, dappled with the burnt umber of fallen leaves. The creek ran crystal clear, the sunlight reflecting off the water with glaring brilliance. Above, the intense blue of a fall sky formed a high arch, marred only by an occasional white cloud. The distinctive scent of autumn mingled with the smoke from the campfire, the silver wisps drifting up through the canopy of color.

Mitch leaned back against the trunk of a massive old cottonwood and drew up one leg, resting his forearm across it. The rough bark penetrated his heavy fisherman knit sweater, and he rubbed against it, scratching his back. Feeling lazy to the bone, he watched his nieces and nephews launch miniature bark canoes in the trickling water, their loud bickering reminding him of years gone by.

The creek was very shallow this time of year, with only a couple of inches of water running over the rocks, but it was still a magnet for the little ones, and Papa Munroe stood guard just a bit downstream, teaching Enrico to fly-fish. Mitch smiled to himself. His stepson was getting pretty darned good and could lay the fly just about anywhere he wanted to.

His attention refocusing on the canoe launch, Mitch grinned again and wondered how long it would be before Murphy's Eric outmaneuvered his cousins, and simply walked into the middle of the stream to get an unobstructed shot at the tiny rapids.

A series of shouts echoed in the open space beyond the tree line, and a loud chorus of dissent rang in the crisp air. The rest of the family was brawling it out in a volleyball game, men against the women. But from the arguing and laughing going on, it sounded as if the women weren't exactly playing by the rules. So everything was pretty much normal.

A shadow fell across him, and without turning his head, he reached up and caught his wife's wrist, tugging her down.

She resisted. "I should go help your mother, Mitchell," she said, her tone scolding. "It is rude to invite them here for a Sunday picnic, then leave her to do all the work." Ignoring her rebuttal, he gave her a firm yank and pulled her down into his lap. Getting her squared away so she was sitting with her back against his chest, he slid his arms under her jacket and around her middle, then hugged her. "My mother doesn't need any help. And she's not working. She's snooping. You watch. She's going to take the lids off everything to see what everyone brought, then she'll sneak little tastes.'' Mitch tucked his head down against Maria's, and they both watched his mother as she started rooting through the containers stacked on the picnic table. True to form, she did exactly what he said she would. "See? I told you."

Maria laughed and snuggled back into his warmth. Resting her head against his shoulder, she covered his hands with hers. "You should not make fun of your mother, Mitchell."

"Hey. I'm not making fun. I'm simply stating facts."

Maria turned her head so her face was pressed against his, and Mitch experienced a rush of recollection, and his chest abruptly constricted.

If he lived to be a hundred, he would never forget that rainy, overcast fall morning ten days ago—when he had staggered into the bathroom and found her standing there, a pregnancy test in her hand, an awestruck expression on her face. And it had taken him a minute for everything to actually sink in. He had been so damned busy the past month, he hadn't even realized she was late. And he would never forget how it felt, to realize they had made a baby together. He still got choked up just thinking about it.

He closed his eyes and tightened his hold, his chest constricting. God, he was so lucky to have her. She had changed his life, and not a day went by that he didn't thank his lucky stars. He honestly didn't know how he had survived without her. And now she had given him the most fantastic gift of all. Yeah, she still drove him crazy, and they still got into the damnedest arguments, but she filled him up. There was just no other way to describe it. Having her in his life changed everything.

He hugged her again, flattening his hand against her abdomen. Pressing his face against hers, he spoke, his voice gruff. "So how are we doing, little mother?"

She hugged his arm, snuggling even deeper into his embrace. Her voice was laced with amusement. "We are doing fine, Mitchell. How are you doing?"

He laughed and hugged her again. "Still spinning I think."

She laughed again and smacked his hand. "You do not spin, Mitchell. You lumber."

Grinning, he rubbed his chin against her hair. He had never heard her use *lumber* before. Must be her new word for the day.

"Mitchell?"

"Hmm?"

"You do not mind that we have not told our families about the baby?"

They hadn't planned on her getting pregnant quite this soon, but when it happened out of the blue, it was such an unexpected surprise that they had both wanted to hoard their happiness for a while. They needed to revel in it—just the two of them. He tightened his hold, reassuring her. "No, darlin'," he responded, his voice husky. "I don't mind at all. I'm not quite ready to share the good news yet, either."

Maria's only response was to press her head back against his shoulder and tighten her arms over his, and he closed his eyes, experiencing another rush. She had totally altered his life, this woman of his.

Even the family get-togethers were tolerable now. He wasn't sure how she did it, but she created a buffer zone somehow, and he didn't dread them like he used to. Of course, it helped that he wasn't getting hassled anymore about his pathetic life. Now they were all picking on Cameron, who had returned from South America. Mitch had all kinds of sympathy for his younger brother.

But there were other changes in his life as well. He had wanted to have Murphy build a big house for them in one of the new subdivisions close to the garden center, but Maria had nearly gone ballistic when he'd brought home some house plans. No house. No move. No way. She was staying right where she was, and if he wanted to live in a new house, he could move out and live in it by himself. Using his most rational tone, he had explained to her that he was getting tired of lugging groceries up the long flight of stairs. Her response was that if he felt that way, he could have all his meals at Joe's Highway Diner.

They'd had one hell of a row all right. But no matter how hard he argued with her, she just could not get it through her head that he wanted to build her a nice new home. And they probably would have still been fighting about it, but she had suddenly burst into tears, sobbing that Fairhaven *was* her beautiful new home. That pretty much finished the argument right then and there.

She did agree, however, that the five of them could not continue living out of two apartments, so they had drawn up plans for major renovations. And as soon as winter set in and business slacked off, Murphy was going to line up contractors to do the work.

"Mitchell?"

He hugged her and rubbed his face against hers. "What?"

"The boys are doing well, are they not? They have adjusted, yes?"

He knew she still worried about them adapting to their new way of life, and even though she could see for herself, she sometimes needed reassurance that she had made the right decision. Smiling, he gave her another squeeze and kissed the side of her neck. "They are so well adjusted, they are more Canadian than most Canadians. And I don't think you could get them to move back to Mexico if you tried to force them."

She clasped his hands and hugged them against her. "You are a good father, Mitchell," she whispered, a thick catch in her voice.

His expression sobering, Mitch flattened one hand against her abdomen again, tucking his head tighter against hers. He'd had no idea he could need anyone the way he needed her. "Mitchell?"

"Yeah?"

She pressed herself tightly against him and whispered, an odd huskiness in her voice. "I think we should go back to our house for a little rest."

Suddenly wanting to laugh, he slid his hand lower, intimately cupping her. He knew exactly where she was going with this. "I thought you were all worried about my mother doing all the work."

Before he had time to get his wits about him, she scrambled up and caught him by the hand. She was standing with her back toward the sun, and a halo of brightness surrounded her, framing her in the light. It made his chest hurt just looking at her.

The wind caught her unbound hair, blowing it across her face, and she quickly tucked it behind her ear. Then she grinned at him and gave a dismissive wave of her hand. "Your mother is not working, Mitchell. You said so yourself." She dug in her heels and started pulling at him, her eyes alight with a scheming look. "Come, Mitchell."

Knowing they would never live it down if they disappeared in the middle of the afternoon—and not quite prepared to give any one of his siblings that kind of ammunition, Mitch figured he'd better turn the tables on her before things got totally out of hand. With lightning speed, he gently put an arm around her knees, so she was sitting down again before she really knew what hit her. She lay down flat on her back.

He grinned down at her, and she gave him a narrow look. "You are not listening to me, Mitchell," she scolded.

Murphy and Jordan appeared on the trail, and Murphy grinned at the pair of them as he draped his arm around his very pregnant wife. "Hey, no wrestling allowed," he said, his voice stern. "You know Ma's rules."

Deciding to dish out a dose of her own medicine, Mitch gave his wife an amused look. "We aren't wrestling," he said. "We're having a debate. I think we should stay here for the picnic, but Maria wants to go home and—"

Before he could get it all out, Maria was up and on her knees behind him, both her hands clamped across his mouth. "Mitchell," she said, laughing, yet managing to sound annoyed. "Your brother does not want to hear about our debates."

His eyes sharp with sudden interest, Murphy nodded. "Yes I do."

Jordan started laughing and caught her husband's hand and turned away. "Come along, dear heart. This is one debate you're staying out of." He frowned at her, but followed her nevertheless. "Why?"

Still grinning, she pulled him along behind her. "Just because."

"What kind of an answer is that?"

As if he were one of their boys, she kept dragging him along. "The only one you're going to get."

Wanting to laugh, but unable to make so much as a sound with Maria's hands clamped across his face, Mitch grasped her wrists and pulled her hands away; then he simply tugged her around to him. Lying in a dazed heap on the ground in front of him, she stared up at him, not quite sure what had happened. He grasped her chin, then leaned down and gave her a kiss. "So, Mrs. Munroe. You still want to go home? And just so you know, if we do go in, I'm going to take my sweet time." He grinned again, holding her gaze. "And you know how demanding you get."

Her hair was spread in a wild tumble on the dried grass, the deep-red of her jacket accentuating the blush in her cheeks, Maria looked up at him, her eyes dancing. She reached up and touched his mouth. "You are such a bad one, husband. And such lies. I do not demand."

Stretching out beside her, Mitch propped his head on his hand and grinned as he lifted some hair away from her face. "Oh, yeah. You do. It's a wonder you don't wake up Grandfather."

Another pink flush crept up her cheeks, but she

lifted her chin in that imperial way of hers. "Grand-father would not hear such things." Then a teasing glint appeared in her eyes, and she began tracing his bottom lip. Then she had the nerve to lecture him. "It would be impolite to leave your family, Mitchell."

Bracing his arm on the other side of her, he leaned down and gave her a long, slow, thorough kiss—one that was hot, wet and deliberate—and definitely not one for public viewing. Her breath caught, and she opened her mouth and grasped his hair, becoming all soft and willing in his arms.

A fog started to form in Mitch's mind, and he abruptly broke off the kiss and got to his feet, pulling her up with him.

Family picnic or not, it was just too bad. There were some things that should not be put off—like making love to your wife in the middle of a perfect autumn afternoon.

Hauling her against him, he started up the path toward the garden center, and Maria slid her arm around his waist and matched him stride for stride. She didn't even argue with him once.

Why would she? This was a marriage of agreement.

* * * * *

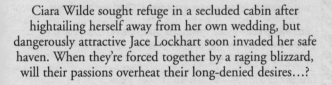
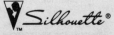

Don't miss Silhouette's newest cross-line promotion,

Four royal sisters find their own Prince Charmings as they embark on separate journeys to find their missing brother, the Crown Prince!

Royally Wed

The search begins in October 1999 and continues through February 2000:

On sale October 1999: **A ROYAL BABY ON THE WAY** by award-winning author **Susan Mallery** (Special Edition)

On sale November 1999: **UNDERCOVER PRINCESS** by bestselling author **Suzanne Brockmann** (Intimate Moments)

On sale December 1999: **THE PRINCESS'S WHITE KNIGHT** by popular author **Carla Cassidy** (Romance)

On sale January 2000: **THE PREGNANT PRINCESS** by rising star **Anne Marie Winston** (Desire)

On sale February 2000: **MAN...MERCENARY...MONARCH** by top-notch talent **Joan Elliott Pickart** (Special Edition)

ROYALLY WED
Only in—
SILHOUETTE BOOKS

Available at your favorite retail outlet.

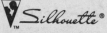

Visit us at www.romance.net

SSERW

MONTANA MAVERICKS
Big Sky Brides

Legendary love comes to Whitehorn, Montana,
once more as beloved authors

Christine Rimmer, Jennifer Greene and Cheryl St.John

present three brand-new stories in this exciting anthology!

Meet the Brennan women:
SUZANNA, DIANA and ISABELLE

Strong-willed beauties who find unexpected
love in these irresistible marriage of
covnenience stories.

Don't miss
MONTANA MAVERICKS: BIG SKY BRIDES
On sale in February 2000,
only from Silhouette Books!

Available at your favorite retail outlet.

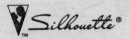